SIMON'S SOUL

SIMON'S SOUL
STANLEY SHAPIRO

G.P. PUTNAM'S SONS • NEW YORK

Copyright © 1977 by Stanley Shapiro
All rights reserved. This book, or parts thereof, must not be reproduced in any form without permission. Published on the same day in Canada by Longman Canada Limited, Toronto.

Library of Congress Catalog Number: 77-6119

SBN: 399-11858-6

PRINTED IN THE UNITED STATES OF AMERICA

*to dear friend Samson,
 who has seen the world for what
 it is and can still smile*

PART I

ONE

July 21 . . .

Dr. Simon Warner has volunteered to be murdered.

For a bachelor, deeply religious, with no close relatives, it was an unselfish, practical decision. It spared the rest of us any emotional scene, such as drawing a short straw or a number out of a hat, although each man would have accepted the role of voyager.

We shall prepare him on a Friday and carry out his death the Saturday that follows. We will, if we succeed, learn if death is an absolute end or if there is something beyond the cessation of physical life, whether it be an unearthly consciousness or a spiritual awareness.

It is a subject that has intrigued the five of us for many years. In our late forties and early fifties, we are chronologically at the right age to discuss death. Not so young that it is too far in the future to contemplate seriously or so old that it is too close to the present to discuss comfortably.

Stanley Shapiro

It had all begun as casual after-dinner conversation. With no surgery the following morning, we could relax late into the night, secure behind expensive cigars and expansive brandy. Each man could share part of his fears, fantasies, and faith. From comfortable, idle conjecture, it had evolved into theories, challenges, and, finally, an obligation to laboratory-test our summations, to prove or disprove them scientifically. Whereas at the beginning we each had gingerly put a toe into the pool of death, secure in the knowledge that we could withdraw that appendage at will, we were now obsessed with the idea of immersing ourselves completely, of slipping from shallow speculation into the deep waters of fact.

Though physicians and surgeons, we do not really know what happens when life stops, simply because science does not really know what life is. We do not really know what happens when death starts, because we do not really know what death is.

We try to save a life, and, failing, we pronounce the person dead. They are taken away and prepared for burial. If there is a God and a Beyond, then we have done our professional best. If there is nothing, then medicine and society are derelict in not doing more to protect man's only treasure, his life. If there is nothing beyond life, then to live should be the ultimate social goal. Every effort must be dedicated to preserving that life, to compress Heaven into seventy earthly years.

If there *is* something beyond death, then man's deeds and his nature can be tolerated, for what is a momentary indiscretion compared to an immortal consecration?

SIMON'S SOUL

In all our discussions, we agreed on that point, that neither medicine nor the church examines death too closely. We rush the deceased from hospital to mortuary to church service to grave too quickly. If there is a soul or a spirit, it is at the precise moment of death that it begins its existence, but it is the last thing the physician or the minister is concerned with. The physician tries to bring life back to the body, and the minister tries to bring the family back to the church. But what has happened to the deceased? Did his spirit or soul or ghost depart? And if so, where to? How does one communicate with a dead person to learn whether his death is oblivion or a step forward?

Over a period of time, we had consulted mediums, mystics, and psychics. In many dozens of sessions, we saw no ghosts, heard no voices, felt no presence.

The senior of our group, Dr. Leonard Carlson, in numerous experiments with dogs, had kept the canine brain functioning after death by providing a flow of fresh blood and oxygen. The electronic monitoring devices had shown brain activity long after all other bodily organs had ceased to function. What he had done with dogs, we proposed to do with a human.

If, at the precise instant of physical death, we could maintain brain function, the dead man could be aware of what was happening to him. Aware that he was dead, possibly aware of any spiritual or soul transition.

Dr. Stuart Blakely, during a craniotomy, having triangulated the skull area of the patient, having inserted the electrodes into the frontal and temporal lobes, watching the brain-wave reaction on stereotaxic instruments and electroencephalograph monitors, found the patient unable to respond verbally to his questions. It is normal for a surgeon to talk to a patient during certain types of brain surgery. The type of response, the speed of response, the clarity of speech, of thought, is of vital importance. Dr. Blakely asked the patient to *think* certain words. Since all brain action creates brain waves, these waves were recorded on the monitors. Afterward, feeding the recorded waves into a differential computer, Dr. Blakely was made aware that each word thought formed a different wave.

"Like fingerprints," he said. "If we could actually feed the human language into a man's brain and have him think the words back, we would have a separate wave for each word. We could put those waves into a computer for decoding. We could create a language of thoughts."

Whereas man's dreams jump from illusion to illusion, hope to hope, belief to belief, science must proceed one step at a time. Religion has never bridged the gap between life and death. It has never *proved* a beyond-death existence. Mystics and mediums—not to cast doubts on them or their methods—had never given us anything concrete, only their word and the word of a few followers, who could well have been hallucinating.

We will take the first logical and most important step into death. That of retaining communication with the dead man.

TWO

August 27 . . .

6:00 A.M. . . . I awake before my family. It is the one advantage of being a surgeon. You do not see too much of them. No matter how deeply a man may love his wife, four or five consecutive hours is the maximum stress any marital partner can put on the other without the situation becoming repetitious.

She sleeps quietly, one of her many virtues. The middle daughter of a middle-class midwestern family . . . sowed with conservative Baptist seeds, raised and readied by a chauvinist creed, harvested by a young doctor out of St. Louis.

Blond hair to her waist, green eyes, sculpted nose, perfect teeth, soft lips, full breasts crowned with pink nipples. Small of waist, golden pubic hairs guarding self-lubricating gates that gracefully open to welcome her husband again and again and once again. Shapely, firm legs that faithfully embrace her mate to please and please and please again.

Never mind that she is not too bright. She is smart enough to have a drink and dinner ready when I come home. Never mind that she cares naught for politics and less for philosophy. The house is clean, the bed sheets fresh, the bathroom prepared.

Never mind that the waters of her social level rise no higher than the supermarket and the beauty salon. She will sit on the edge of the bed in a sheer, sweet-smelling nightgown and massage the world's tensions out of my neck and back.

In her simplicity, she has achieved a totality. At forty-two, she looks thirty-two. After eighteen years of marriage, she still enters the bed like a virgin. Women's liberation is a battle being fought in distant, godless countries.

There are women who, by pleasing men, please themselves . . . who, by serving, become the served . . . who, by giving, accumulate.

Never mind that her simplicity ofttimes tires my patience. She will never test my patriarchy. The surgeon has neither the time nor the temper to test new theorems. The sharpened blade in his hand, the obedient assisting doctors and nurses, the helpless patient, the hush before the incision, his absolute superiority, a white-gowned, gauze-covered majesty. How can one live among the gods in the morning and only as an equal at night? I married the right woman.

SIMON'S SOUL

I caress her breasts as she sleeps. She makes low, sweet, satisfied sounds. How much more pleasant to the ear than the practical spoken words if she were awake. "What would you like for dinner? . . . Shall I invite the Jamisons? . . . Tommy's teacher said he is not doing well in math." All bits of trivia that a surgeon who is off to remove a piece of lung that morning can do without.

When a man sees how fragile life is, the more irritable fragile remarks make him. Each morning I go from the breakfast table to a life-and-death table in the operating room. If you are going to talk to me, talk important. I don't give a damn that Tommy's math is bad. He's either going to be the world's greatest football player—he can throw a football sixty yards into a barrel—or he's going to be the stud of the western hemisphere. He is literally hung like the proverbial horse. I don't know how he can get it all into any woman. How can I tell my wife that her sixteen-year-old baby has made it with three of her best friends and five of their best daughters . . . that he's been offered money, apartments, and cars for his favors? When you're hung like a horse, it doesn't matter that you add and subtract like a horse.

Long hours, early to bed and early to rise, do not make the surgeon wise or his wife contented. Sex becomes, if you will excuse the expression, an on-again, off-again situation. Hit or miss, now and then, from one extreme to the other. Life is part celebration, part celibacy. I've read novels about the sexual exploits of medical men, all obviously written by nonmedical men. I do not have sex

Stanley Shapiro

with my patients. It's difficult to become aroused over a woman on whom you're performing a mastectomy or from whom you're removing a uterus.

I would imagine a physician-patient relationship that extends into the bedroom might exist in the analytical field. I can see a psychiatrist deciding that the best way to treat a nympho is to give her some of her own medicine. But blood and scalpeled flesh are not aphrodisiacs.

As the human body lies there, cut open, parts removed, my thoughts are not of conquest but of contemplation. I am torn between religion and reality, trying to make both one entity. I want to see eternity, I see extinction. The here and now is so final, the Hereafter so flimsy. Is there life after death? Was there something before life? Is there a God, or is it all a goddamned lie?

I am soul-searching in every sense of the phrase. All of us in this project are obsessed with the same questions. What is so frustrating is that there is an answer to everything. How big is the universe? What is it? How did it start? Is there life on other planets? Is there a Hereafter? There are absolute, definite answers to each and every question. Man just doesn't know them. But there *are* answers, and the instinct to find them has overwhelmed us.

I have not scheduled any office appointments or surgery for the next several days. The others in the group have done the same.

I go to the kitchen to prepare some coffee, and I encounter my son. I curse science for not having perfected the pill seventeen years ago. How could I have planted this mute, defiant, parasitic seed in my wife's

SIMON'S SOUL

womb? How could she have nourished this ungrateful embryo into infancy? How could she have released it to the world to bear my name?

He sits there eating some monstrous sandwich and drinks milk straight from the bottle, the white froth riding above his thick upper lip.

He is still fully dressed. That means he has just come home. Somewhere some woman sleeps peacefully, with a throbbing vagina inducing the dream of dreams, and in my kitchen the dream sits and devours new energy. He is a muscular six feet, with a rugged, ordinary face that does not mask a rugged, ordinary brain. But that brain knows it has a tremendous cock, and it is learning to use it, not as an instrument of pleasure but as a weapon with which to divide and conquer. His superiority lies in his nakedness, and since naked we all approach the bed, his will be done.

Those extra inches, in an infinite universe, make him a finite ruler—and he will rule with that fleshly scepter, in a growing, adoring kingdom, without wisdom, without compassion. Like so many other sporting games, it is a game of inches. Never will he have to labor or want, or be turned away. He will conquer where mightier and more brilliant men fail. He will accumulate their most prized possessions merely by dropping his pants. If there is a Hereafter, the revenge of eternity will be if it is sexless.

I will try to be civil in the house my enemy shares. "Good morning."

"Uh huh." A mumble comes out, eluding chopping teeth and chopped food.

The slightest sound from this healthy hulk is like

putting a match to a fuse. "What do you mean, 'uh huh?' Can't you say good morning?"

"Uh huh."

"Damn it, stop chewing like a horse and talk like a person. 'Uh huh' is not 'good morning.'" He hunches over like a gigantic penguin. He is weighing the alternatives—telling me to go fuck myself, against an always full refrigerator.

The glutton masters the oaf. "Good morning," he mumbles into the table.

"You want to stay out all night, fine. Just get yourself a job, an apartment, clothes, food, a car, and be your own man."

He chews sullenly. Just another two years and it will be legal for him to let some woman keep him.

I look at him—his appearance, his manners, his hours—and I take the offensive behind those old standby words, "After all the things I gave you."

He takes shelter behind the equally old standby, "I never asked you for anything."

I blurt out, "You never told me to stop."

His orgasm-glazed eyes suddenly look stupidly into mine, as the thought, like a ferret, scurries through his maze of brain cells. Triumphantly, I hang on to that magnificent answer and unforeseen weapon. *You never told me to stop.* Why hadn't I thought of that years ago? "Why didn't you say, 'Dad, I'm sixteen; stop giving me things; let me get off my fat ass and earn them'?"

I am out of the house before he can answer. It isn't often that a father can leave a confrontation with him victorious.

SIMON'S SOUL

I leave my home and drive east through Westwood, until a few years ago a charming college village of movie houses and coffeehouses, drugstores, shoestores, and bookstores, shops that sold junk at a price and others that called them antiques and sold them as a prize. A thousand one-story shops for the student body to crawl over. Secure behind their Westwood Wall, peering out from behind books and professors, a month of meals in every check from home—if not the best years of their lives, certainly the least worrisome.

And now the suspect establishment has invaded Westwood and planted its poisonous seeds in the ground, and from tiny architects' plans mighty buildings grow—twenty- and thirty-story monsters spring up out of the ground like thick turds, looking down on the student body with all the enthusiasm of a mortician gazing at a pauper. Progress will turn this campus into a midnight danger zone. It will empty the sidewalk of that most majestic sight, the solitary stroller.

East into Beverly Hills and to what one can't ignore, the banks, one on every corner, silent sentinels of an affluent society. Small shops climbing toward elegance but never quite reaching it. Shops that desperately cling to the ledge of respectability, just a drop away from falling into outright cheapness. An exclusive discotheque next door to a five-and-dime store, a wine-and-cheese shop catering in high prices across the street from a delicatessen catering in high blood pressure. One-hundred-dollar-a-day hotel rooms that look over a railroad track you would find in any small midwestern town. And, finally, the treasured, tenured tenants, that city's chosen people, the psychia-

19

Stanley Shapiro

trists. Beverly Hills is their anthill, and they crawl within its steel-structured body. Fall into any office at random and the chances are a psychiatrist will pick you up. Stand outside any building at five minutes to the hour and watch the changing of the patients. Beverly Hills, banks and psychiatrists, vaults and valium. Security of mind and money.

Up Coldwater Canyon, that long, twisting road to the mountaintop, and over into the valley below. On each side of the road $150,000 homes flush against one another. Poshness without privacy. Live in one, listen to your wealthy neighbors argue. The golden ghetto.

To the top of the canyon and left on Mulholland Drive. Wilderness takes over. Secluded homes surrounded by forest and fire hazard.

Isolated earthly fortresses containing jaded superstars and faded old stars. Walled-up legends, the In-Group keeping out their admirers, the Out-Group keeping in their memories. Bigger than life, they strip the life around them. They have carved into the very guts of the mountain itself, pulling out a thousand trees as if they were so many decaying teeth, sending the animal life scurrying to the concrete death below. They have filled the raw, bleeding cavities with superhomes for their superegos. Decorated wastelands. Million-dollar monuments to their psyches—with muscled chauffeurs, silicone-breasted mistresses, and giant watchdogs to assure them they are indeed what they indeed are not. And on full-moon, cocaine-inspired, savage nights, master, mistress, chauf-

SIMON'S SOUL

feur and sometimes dog share the beds on which kings once slept. Neither ironic nor sacrilegious, for the kings too had their servants and ladies and beasts. History never surprises itself, it only repeats itself.

Dr. Warner is a medical stranger in this celluloid paradise. His house, a tree-enclosed, fence-protected Spanish estate, built in the twenties by a recluse, the only son of an early film magnate's only marriage. With rugs and furnishings, tiles and tapestries, shipped from Spanish castles—shades drawn to protect yesterday's glories from today's sun eye—this recluse son spent his years in only three of the two dozen rooms. Surrounded by ancient literature and still older depressions, the recluse son went from recluse to eccentric to psychotic to senile to dead.

Just as some are born to suffer, this home was born to shelter the suffering. It would know only the steps of uncertainty, anxiety, despair, and unfulfilled dreams. Never the swift, light sounds of children's feet, never the laughter of husband and wife, never the warmth of family life. This sad, Spanish house. From recluse son to recluse doctor. But whereas the isolated son had been content to die without being observed, the isolated doctor now planned to die and tell all.

Dr. Warner, a man who has earned large sums of money, with no family to dissipate it on, has put it back into his lifework. His basement has, over the years, been converted into a functioning surgery room. With his own funds and with grants from foundations to conduct research, he has equipment the equal of that of any advanced hospital. It is in this room we will conduct the experiment. It is here we will learn if Dr. Warner has a soul or a spirit. We cannot search for the soul of a dog or a guinea pig. Only a human will do. Only a human can tell us.

8:00 A.M. . . . We are all assembled in the operating room. Myself, Dr. Warner, Dr. Carlson, Dr. Blakely, and Dr. Steven Mannis. Our first task will be to implant the language into Dr. Warner's brain, have him think the words back, record the wave marks they make, feed them into the computer so it can later decipher the thoughts.

We shave Dr. Warner's skull, preparing for the craniotomy. We mark off the areas where the electrodes will be inserted, and the triangulation begins. All stereotaxic instruments, stimulators and recorders, electroencephalograph monitors, are functioning. The X-ray monitor helps us locate the frontal and temporal lobes of the cerebral cortex, which control thought, memory, and speech.

The computer, into which we have fed the dictionary's words, now begins to feed the words into Dr. Warner's memory center. They are fed in at an incredible rate of speed, for the brain can absorb monumental amounts of information at one time. His thought center sends the words back in wave form. The waves are transferred from the electroencephalograph machine to the computer, which decodes the word from the wave and stores it for future use. Each word thought has become a fingerprint.

3:00 P.M. . . . We have completed our input of words and its identification feedback. We have tested the blood and oxygen machines that we will hook up to Dr. Warner to feed his brain after we have cut off his normal supply. Tomorrow morning we will kill him.

8:00 P.M. . . . The five of us have a dinner of beef stew, which Dr. Carlson has cooked. Dr. Warner sits there, his head shaved and marked off beneath the protective stocking cap. He is quiet, composed, like Christ. The others eat lightly, nervously, like his disciples. I think deep down we each feel a little guilty, a little relieved, that it is he who is going to die and not we.

That night I have sex with my wife. My mind is on the next morning and not on satisfying her. I find I perform in superlative fashion for two hours. The less I care to prove myself, the more I prove. Why does sex have to be victory or defeat? Why does man have to feel triumphant? Why does mastery replace satisfaction? Why is the woman's orgasm more important to the man than his own? Why is his partner's joy a symbol of his own? I do not feel my wife's orgasm, I do not experience the pleasure of it, and yet without it I have failed. Instead of pleasing ourselves, we are continually testing ourselves. Why does our masculinity lie in their femininity?

August 28. . .

8:30 A.M. . . . We all arrive at Dr. Warner's home. He is dressed in dark blue pajamas and a yellow silk robe, and carries a small hand Bible. He is probably the most religious man of us all. In a short while he will call that Bible to account.

The guilts and anxieties of the previous day have

Stanley Shapiro

disappeared. We are now stimulated. On an emotional high. We are challenging eons of ignorance. We are opening the door that leads to eternal light or eternal darkness. We are so anxious that, and I am ashamed to say it, if Dr. Warner wanted to back out, it is conceivable we might not let him do so.

8:55 A.M. ... We all descend into the basement and into the operating room in silence. There is nothing more to say. Dr. Warner, holding the Bible, gets on his knees, says a short, silent prayer, kisses the Bible, rises, shakes our hands. He has one last speech as a living being. "If there is something beyond, then I am alive forever. If not, what does an extra twenty years on earth matter? We're alive so short and dead so long."

He removes his bathrobe, his pajama top, and lies down on the table, Bible in hand. Like millions of others who have faced death, he has an unshakable belief in God. We will soon see if there is a God to have an unshakable belief in.

10:40 A.M. ... We have again triangulated. The electrodes are in their proper place inside the brain. They are recording into our monitors and our computers. We ask Dr. Warner not to talk aloud, just to think. He thinks. The waves go from monitor into computer, where the waves are decoded, and the computer sends out the slip of paper on which are his thoughts: "There *is* something beyond death. ... I am not afraid. ... Please proceed."

11:05 A.M. ... Dr. Warner has been rendered physically unaware. We use the computer to feed our questions to him. Is he in pain? "No, there is no pain. ... But I cannot

SIMON'S SOUL

feel. Is the Bible still in my hands?" We assure him it is.

11:15 A.M. . . . "Simon, we are ready to transfer you onto the oxygen and blood machines."

"Yes, go ahead."

"Your body and your brain will continue to function, but separately from each other."

"I understand."

"We cannot reverse the process."

"I'm aware of that."

"Shall we proceed?"

"Please open the Bible to Revelations."

We open the Bible to the page it begins on.

"Revelations is in your hands."

"Thank you. I am ready."

12:05 P.M. . . . He is hooked up. The machines are supplying blood and oxygen to his brain, independent of the rest of his body.

"We are now going to inject twenty-five cc's of insulin into your vein, which will cause your heart to stop."

"Yes, I know."

"Dr. Mannis will count to ten. Right after ten, you will be dead."

"I understand."

Dr. Blakely has inserted the needle into his vein. Dr. Mannis counts into the computer, which counts to Dr. Warner. "One . . . two . . . three . . . four . . . five . . . six . . . seven . . . eight . . . nine . . . ten."

Dr. Blakely injects the insulin. Dr. Warner's heart stops. He is dead. The computer sends out his thoughts. "I am dead. . . . I felt no pain. . . . I cannot hear or see or

Stanley Shapiro

talk or move.... I am dead, but I can think.... It is all darkness.... No shadow.... No light.... But I am aware that my body is dead."

This is the moment, the transition from life to death. The moment when soul and spirit and Hereafter become fact or fiction. Have we killed a man and our theories, or have we given new life to him and knowledge to ourselves? Have we taken a step into the unknown, or is it the end of all steps, and all that exists is the known?

The computer continues to decode his thoughts. "Nothing but darkness.... Not a sea of darkness, just a tight coil of it.... I cannot see beyond it or think beyond it.... I can only wait."

When does the soul depart? When does the spirit rise? When does God take over? If there is just darkness, then he is simply a dead man who is still thinking, and if the brain is left to die, then there is nothing left. Then we have killed a man to prove what so many people have so long felt, that there is nothing after death. I feel a tremendous sorrow for mankind.

Dr. Warner's dead hands clutch the Bible.

"There has to be something," Dr. Carlson whispers fiercely.

"That's the chance he took," Dr. Blakely answers quietly, never taking his eyes off Dr. Warner. "All or nothing."

12:11 P.M.... Dr. Warner has been medically dead for six minutes, and the computer continues to record. "It's dark.... Nothing, nothing.... I'm still in my body.... I don't know how to get out ... or where to go.... Nowhere to go ... It's dark."

SIMON'S SOUL

"Damn it." Dr. Mannis bites the words. "Oblivion."

A nagging optimism sends soft jabs into my gut. "Oblivion means absolute nothingness. Darkness is not nothingness. It's merely a lack of light."

"Only because his mind is still functioning, Ben," replies Dr. Mannis. "So he imagines darkness. Kill the brain and it will be oblivion."

I can't accept it. "It took Christ three days to rise. Why should we expect miracles in six minutes? If there's a spirit or a soul that leaves after death, how can it leave while his mind still remains? The mind is the essence of the man."

Dr. Mannis feeds the question into the computer, which transfers it to Dr. Warner. "Do you think we are holding you back by keeping your brain functioning?"

"I don't know.... There is only darkness, and an awareness you are back there."

"Back where, Simon?"

"Where I once was ... Alive ... I know I can never return.... But I do not know where I am supposed to go.... Hold on to me.... Don't let me go yet."

"Why not?"

"Because ... there may be nothing ... and I'm frightened.... Don't let me go."

12:14 P.M. ... Dr. Warner has been dead for nine minutes. We are all despondent. From the emotional high, we have crashed to a shattering low. Souls and spirits and ghosts. Heaven and Hell. God and Satan. All fantasies of mortal man, who fears mortality, so he has created something beyond to ease everything here.

1:32 P.M. ... "Darkness ... nothing but darkness."

"God almighty," sighs Dr. Mannis.

"That's odd," says Dr. Blakely. "You're saying God almighty as we sit here confronted with the very fact that there is no God almighty."

It is odd how old habits hang on. I cannot shake the feeling that somehow we are to blame for this seeming impasse. That we have opened a door for Dr. Warner but not allowed him to walk through it. That by holding on to his mind, we act as an uncut umbilical cord, preventing him from leaving the parent to face his new life. I mention my thoughts to the others, and we pose the question to Dr. Warner. Shall we let him go?

"I don't know . . . I don't know. Hold on. Just a little longer." In an incredibly desperate situation he is reacting with admirable reason. In his position, he can be excused his indecisiveness more than we who hover over his dead body.

2:43 P.M. . . . "Darkness . . . nothing but darkness."

We are all exhausted. The exhilaration of attacking the unknown has given way to the fatigue of facts. Considering our goals, we have fallen far short, but taken in proper perspective, we have leaped scientific millennia. We are communicating with a dead man. There are a handful of Nobel prizes in that alone, but we shall never lay claim to them.

Our problem now lies in what to do with the brain that rests in a hulk that is starting to deteriorate. We will have to turn off the machines and dispose of the body as planned.

SIMON'S SOUL

"We will have to turn off the machines, Simon."

And the anguished answer, "No, please, not yet."

We are now prisoners of the dead man. How can we turn away from someone who is out there alone, who has given up his life to prove there is nothing beyond it?

4:17 P.M.... With his body in a slightly inclined position, his abdominal cavity is beginning to swell as his blood collects there. Body gases further distort him. Urine and fecal matter have come out of his body. We have cleaned it up. His body is deteriorating, but his brain is functioning. It is being properly oxygenated. But there are limits even to that. As the body cells and tissues and flesh break down, they will contaminate the brain. This entire experiment was based on the moments after death, not on keeping the brain alive for a prolonged period of time.

I turned to Dr. Mannis. "Tell Simon we have to discontinue the experiment."

The message is sent, and the answer comes back, "No, not yet! I feel more than darkness.... Like waves or ripples in it ... Like something is trying to get through!"

THREE

Something more than darkness. Like waves or ripples. It is a devastating message.

Dr. Carlson's words at first seem unbelievable, coming from him. "He's lying." We all just stare at him. "He doesn't want us to cut off the machines."

"What has he got to gain by lying?"

"Time."

"Time for what?"

"To hold on."

"Hold on to what?"

"Us ... life ... something. Anything is better than nothing."

My God, are we arguing whether to give a dead man another few minutes of our time? Has the failure of the experiment so unnerved us that each man is now thinking not of the cosmos but of the courts? We've committed no crime. We've researched a subject that the church and medicine should have been working on a long time ago.

SIMON'S SOUL

"Maybe he is lying," I cry out. "Wouldn't you? He's out there alone. Forever. If there is nothing, why shouldn't he hold on? What's a few minutes to us? To him that's his eternity."

I feel a sense of closeness, of oneness, with Dr. Warner. He truly is alone, but then we all are. We surround ourselves with jobs and wives and children to create a sense of well-being, of belonging, of being necessary. But the job, the wife, the child, are all an illusion of our immortality syndrome. They exist only in life, vanish in death. If I died, there would be no more physician. My wife would soon be the wife of another. My son would pursue his own pleasures, with an occasional fleeting thought about a father he never knew too well. There was only one person who truly needed me, whose very existence hung on my good faith, Dr. Warner. We were one. He was now somewhere where I would be in a few years. He was sailing a dark ocean, trying to chart a course for me. Could I abandon the man who had given his life to give me knowledge?

"I do not believe he is lying," I say, and I know I am right. "A man who has the courage to die will not start to lie to preserve that which is already lost."

6:10 P.M. . . . We have drained the blood from Dr. Warner's body, packed ice around the body for temporary preservation.

"We have drained your blood, Simon."

"Yes. Good."

"We have packed your body in ice."

"Yes. Thank you."

"Do you still feel the waves?"

"Like ripples in the darkness. Like a black pulse."

"Has it a rhythmical beat?"

"It's irregular ... There ... I felt it now. ... Like a gentle bump ... Now nothing. ... Just darkness ... There it is again. ... Now nothing."

Dr. Blakely, his face drawn in concern, sits down on a chair, lights a cigarette, inhales the smoke as though it were a life-sustaining food and liquid force, then, almost reluctantly, lets the soothing smoke out of his body. "This sort of pulse beat," he theorizes. "Let's say he's not hallucinating. Can't they just be thought waves? After all, we *are* communicating with him. Maybe they're just the energy waves of communication."

It is a sobering theory, because it is quite possible.

To test the validity of this theory, we inform Dr. Warner that we will not communicate with him for two minutes. In two minutes we will again contact him, and he can tell us if the wavelengths diminished without communication.

6:12 P.M. ... We stand in silence around the body. All is quiet except for the soft sound of the machines pumping blood and oxygen, keeping brain cells and tissues alive.

In those one hundred and twenty seconds, I see the four men, one dead and three alive, with a clarity of perception I had never had before. Even with our dearest friends, we go through life seeing only the qualities that make them dear to us. Either we overlook the blemishes, or we enlarge them out of proportion. If we're against

SIMON'S SOUL

homosexuality, then the fact that a person is one becomes the entire entity. We do not hear his thoughts or honor his abilities. All we can say is, "John? He's a fag."

Why hadn't I noticed before that Dr. Carlson was more than just a senior in years, a man whose aid you sought in knotty medical problems, who saw your patients when you were on vacation, who played a fair game of golf and was married to an opinionated harpy? I should have known more that that about him.

His graying hairs clung tenaciously to his scalp. Brown eyes seemed to stare at all things at once. A face lined not by laughter but by tension and age. His three capped teeth easy to distinguish from his real ones. A stomach that he kept trying to suck in. Just as youth has an aura of vitality, whether real or imaginary, age has an aura of decay, never imaginary. Dr. Carlson was decaying, and he knew it. The physician in him accepted a beginning, a middle, and an end. The Catholic in him reached for something beyond the end. I am sorry that I had been harsh with him. He was torn between protecting the good name of a lifetime's work and seeking forbidden information on a future that was coming alarmingly close. For some reason, he wore a dark brown mustache. Perhaps he kept it because it didn't turn gray, but it gave him a villainous smile. It made a straight nose look like a sharp nose. It made him look like a paunchy, sly, uncaring hawk. Housed in the hawk was the best surgeon I had ever met, and the most compassionate. A patient in pain, and he suffered. A patient dead, and he went to the funeral. The surgeon at the gravesite. It always gave onlookers the wrong idea. The mustache turned his grief into a leering smile and produced endless gossip. A decent man. If there is an afterlife, he is most deserving of a good one.

Dr. Stuart Blakely. At fifty-one, a brilliant, cold-blooded son of a bitch. He would be thinking of dinner while a patient was on a heart-lung machine. He walked away from death as casually as one does from a skinned knee, knowing the inner peace of not being at fault. But better Dr. Blakely than an inept samaritan. I have seen cold gray eyes before, but none that looked as if they had just been taken out of the freezer and inserted into their sockets. They didn't look at you, they photographed you. It was rumored by neighbors that he played the piano every night upon returning home. If it was Chopin, the patient had lived. If it was Wagner, the patient had died. You couldn't put your life into better, more expensive hands. A muscular man who took care of his body with the same professional detachment with which he treated his patients. Twice a husband, thrice a father. He flew a plane, scuba dived, skied, and mountain climbed, but never discussed it. He lived a full life unemotionally.

Dr. Steven Mannis. The baby of the group at forty-two. The typical bearded Jewish liberal we gentiles always hear about. His father martyred to tailordom to send him to medical school. His mother martyred to her son. The son martyred to his guilt that two parents could destroy their identities to give him his. And striking back at them, by striking at the stabilizing social forces they represented, law, tradition, pride. A doctor by training, a

SIMON'S SOUL

religious man by instinct, a revolutionary by reaction. With a black wife, a half-black son, snubbing his nose at the establishment while driving the best cars it could produce. Supporting his parents while ignoring them. Brittle but terribly bright. Contemptuous but very courageous.

Dr. Simon Warner. All six feet and one hundred and seventy pounds of him. The Wasp who made America great. The ones who crossed huge oceans in small ships and endless prairies in battered wagons. Who tilled their fields of its food and their minds for its creations. Who built churches and schools and hospitals and cities. Who invented electric lights and telephones, automobiles and airplanes. Phonographs and television, atom bombs and vaccines. The white European, who crossed frontiers as casually as others would go to visit a neighbor. Who built cities in the desert, and will build them on distant planets. The blond, blue-eyed symbol of oppression to minorities but a constant salvation to mankind. The twentieth century rode on his back, his mind, and his spirit.

With the same dedication, he had volunteered to cross the final frontier. With the same superior spirit, he calmly went off on the last of man's possible adventures. That has been the dual strength of the white man. Dedication and the ability to function as part of a group while still retaining individual thought. He lies there dead, blood drained, body packed in ice, but he is still part of the team.

I do not know too much about his personal life, except

Stanley Shapiro

that he was born in Iowa, was a bachelor reputed to have a fair stable of women, drank moderately, gambled occasionally, practiced his profession carefully, and died bravely.

I cannot and will not abandon him until all efforts are exhausted and all have failed.

6:14 P.M. . . . We turn the computers and monitors on again. Dr. Mannis advises Dr. Warner we are in communication again. Has he felt any further waves?

"Yes."

It is an electrifying word. Either they are self-induced waves of a mind that is still emitting energy, or there is more than just darkness out there. There is a force! Something, something. We ask him to try to explain it.

"It's out there, beyond the darkness."

Triumph! Exhilaration! He has said it is beyond the darkness! He has separated the darkness from the force!

"It's more than just ripples. . . . It's as though something were beating against the darkness to reach me."

My skin grows cold; slivers of fear go through me. Something is trying to reach him. "Ask him"—I pursue the reasoning that will not leave me—"ask him again if by holding his mind we are holding him prisoner. Perhaps the darkness is the remains of life, and beyond the darkness is the Hereafter. Perhaps if we destroy his mind, we will destroy the darkness."

The question is asked. The answer is firm, professional. "It may be, but we mustn't cut off. The purpose of my dying wasn't just to learn whether there's an afterlife, but to be able to relate it to you."

It's odd how a dead man, in a terrifying situation, can

SIMON'S SOUL

be more rational than we who are gathered around him. I think a man reaches a point where there is absolutely nothing else he can do—no other choice he can make—where he must accept the situation. He is more apt to make rational decisions than those who have options open, who can contemplate alternatives. He cannot withdraw, advance, change, or decide. Just accept. With absolutely no control over the situation, he can be more objective than we who are filled with hopes and fears, opinions, theories, and anxieties.

"It's all around me. . . . It's hammering at the darkness, like fists against a velvet curtain."

Like fists against a velvet curtain. A curtain. A curtain that, lifted, may reveal the millenium's secrets, the answer to the unanswerable, the solution to the unsolvable, the reality of the dream, the truth of the hope.

I am in a state of controlled excitement. I cap my hope as one would the top of a volcano. It will eventually explode in disappointment or discovery.

The scientist in me says it may still be his own energy waves or the waves of our communicating with him. He is nothing but a mind now, sensitive only to waves of energy. The electrical discharges would beat like a surf against the dark void he is in, like a fist on a velvet curtain.

But it just may be, it just may be that there *is* something beyond the darkness. If it is nothing but energy, not created by us or by him, that alone is a triumph. Then death is not oblivion. Energy, even raw, is force, and force is the opposite of nothingness.

Dr. Blakely comes up with a logical deduction that has

escaped me in the excitement. Perhaps the pulsations, the waves, the fist on the velvet curtain, are an attempt at communication, some sort of code.

"I don't know," thinks back Dr. Warner. "I don't think it is a message. Why would anything try to contact me in a circle, from all sides?"

Again the rational thinking of a man who has no choice but to be rational.

"Try to contact it, Simon. Try to think to it."

Dr. Warner thinks, and we also receive the message of his mind. "My name is Dr. Simon Warner. I am a human. I have just died. I do not know where I am. If you understand me, please contact me by stopping the waves I feel coming at me. Then let me be aware of three long waves, followed by three short waves."

He repeats this thought over and over, countless times, until we begin to become impatient with the repetition. But then, what if he repeats it a million times? What can he lose? Where is he going? What else has he got to do? Another awareness of his situation balanced against ours. We, with our hours and days to be accounted for. He, with no more concept of or concern with time, just with continuity.

7:20 P.M. . . . Dr. Warner is still trying to make contact. Each of us will take fifteen minutes to go upstairs, get a sandwich, go to the bathroom, and make any necessary phone calls. As I urinate, the juxtaposition of my acts is ironic. I am taking an ordinary, everyday pee, and in the basement below we are trying to contact eternity.

I call my wife and tell her I will not be home that

SIMON'S SOUL

night. I am working with an associate on a case. She is quite used to that.

I make a quick sandwich from a refrigerator Dr. Warner wisely left well stocked. His maid has been given a week off. His phone is answered by a service. Not that I expect anyone to come by. A recluse in life, he is not likely to be disturbed in death. . . . Food and phones and maids and bathrooms. Such earthly trivialities. Alone in this gigantic universe, we worry whether an answering service picked up a call for us. Alive for seventy years, dead for billions of years, we are outraged that our taxes have gone up.

7:45 P.M. . . . I return to the operating room. Dr. Carlson takes his break. Dr. Warner is still trying to make contact. Come late evening, we will take turns sitting with Dr. Warner's body while the others sleep.

8:30 P.M. . . . "Are the fists still beating on the curtain, Simon?"

"Yes, but it doesn't feel as if they are trying to break through."

"What does it feel like?"

"Helpless anger . . . Frustrated urgency."

Dr. Blakely presses for information. "You have used words that puzzle us. Fists and anger. It makes whatever is beyond the curtain seem violent."

"I don't feel the violence. . . . At least, not yet . . . But I do feel anger."

"Then the curtain, the darkness, would be a protection from whatever is beyond it?"

"In a way, protective. In a way, a harmful barrier."

"Harmful? In what way, Simon?"

"I can't explain. Whatever is beyond needs to reach me."

"You mentioned frustrated urgency."

"Yes. Urgency . . . That's the best word."

"Why is it urgent?"

"I don't know. . . . It's like when you have to catch a train that is pulling out of the station. You mustn't miss it . . . mustn't miss it . . . mustn't miss it."

I can feel the perspiration wetting the hairs on the back of my neck.

"Miss what, Simon?"

"I don't know, but I mustn't miss it. . . . I can't get to it. . . . It can't get to me."

"Because of the curtain?"

"Yes."

Again he chooses words that are pulse jumpers, intoxicating one with the possibilities of their meanings. Train station—mustn't miss . . . Trains mean passengers. Trains mean journeys . . . a trip somewhere, and the passengers are souls or spirits. I can feel it in my inner self. Not oblivion, not the end. Thank God. There *is* something. Maybe not God, but something. Thank Something. I've been right all the time. I've been right not to dismiss my instincts. I must tell Dr. Warner. "We are the black curtain, Simon. I think the brain is where the spirit or soul is. You're dead, but your spirit or soul is in your mind. It's here with us. That beating on the curtain . . . It's trying to get your soul, but we have it here."

"Yes, it's possible. . . . I don't know."

SIMON'S SOUL

"It knows you're dead, but there is no soul to take. The train, the station . . . Maybe a soul has an eternal timetable to get to where it is supposed to go. We may be wrong in keeping you. Maybe we should let you go."

A long pause, and then the thought comes back. "Yes, it might be best."

FOUR

We never really expected that answer. He has deliberated, weighed, balanced, and decided. To be let go. To forever and ever be cut off. If there is nothing, to become nothing. If there is something, to go to it without telling us. What incredible power is behind that dark curtain that has the ability to lure him into an unknown eternity? What siren song draws him past the darkness?

A jury of four, with a dead witness whom we have killed, we have to decide. Dr. Carlson and I would let him go. Dr. Mannis is undecided. Dr. Blakely vehemently opposed. I feel we have gone far enough—perhaps further than we have a right to.

Dr. Blakely is disdainful. "The physician has become a parishioner. The researcher, a revivalist. Forget facts, just have blind faith, is that it, Doctor?" he asks derisively.

"The man wants to be let go, Stuart."

"What man?" Dr. Blakely is almost yelling, pointing at

SIMON'S SOUL

the body. "We don't know what it is now. Just a few minutes ago it warned us not to cut him off, and it was right. It feels pulsations, it thinks in terms of railroad stations. It may be the remnants of childhood memories."

"It may also be fact," says Dr. Mannis.

Dr. Blakely grabs that logic as a hawk the chicken. "Exactly. And if it *is* fact, we will not lose the only witness to it. If it's fact, and there *is* eternity, he doesn't need us anymore, but we now need him. If he has a soul and it's going somewhere, he's going to tell us, or he won't go. We now have more to lose than he, and more to gain. We will not terminate the experiment. I did not join in order to abandon."

I can argue with the way he expresses himself, but not with the motivation behind it.

"I don't think the ultimate decision will be ours," Dr. Carlson compromises. "At most we can keep this experiment under control another forty-eight hours. There will be people trying to contact him. People whom *we* have to be in touch with. Medically, contamination will soon set in. We are arguing about forty-eight hours."

I want to be convinced, I want to follow this to its conclusion, but someone must represent Dr. Warner in this earthly courtroom. "We are talking of forty-eight hours *in our lives*. Perhaps *his* forty-eight hours are more important."

"Forty-eight hours important?" Dr. Blakely is almost mocking me. "We're talking about eternity."

"But what if those hours can destroy his eternity?"

"Then that is the chance we and he have to take," Dr. Blakely replies emphatically, emotionlessly. "He died not for comfort but for science."

Of course he is right. We inform Dr. Warner that we do not want to cut off communication.

His thoughts come out of the computer. "I understand."

Midnight . . . We will start to take our two-hour shifts until morning. Three of us will sleep; the fourth will stay with Dr. Warner.

I shower in Dr. Warner's bathroom, shave with his shaving cream and razor, go into the bedroom, and lie down on his bed. Clothes hang neatly in closets. Hairbrushes and books and awards. Jewelry, and clock-radio, and photographs. A lovely blond woman staring from a small picture frame. She probably knew the man and the bedroom far better than I.

We know so little about each other. Even your own psychiatrist won't talk to you more than a couple of times a week, and you're paying him to listen. Who was Simon Warner? Was he that dedicated a researcher or just a man with a death wish, a medical martyr with historical hallucinations? Was he saint, scientist, or psychopath?

1:00 A.M. . . . I am awakened by Dr. Carlson screaming.

I run from the bedroom, across the living room. Dr. Blakely is already descending the stairs to the basement, followed by Dr. Mannis. Down the stairs, along the narrow passageway, into the operating room.

Dr. Blakely stands there, staring, stunned. Dr. Mannis, one hand against the wall to support himself, is retching.

SIMON'S SOUL

Dr. Warner's body lies as we left it, packed in ice, the machines feeding blood and oxygen, the wires leading from his skull to the monitors and computers. Dr. Carlson, or what remains of him, lies a few feet away. His body has been ripped open. Something that could have been done only by a gigantic knife blade or steel claw. Great gashes in his body, which have torn out his inner organs and entrails, scooping chunks of bone and flesh with it. His arm has been literally ripped out of its socket and torn loose. It lies a few feet from the body. Blood everywhere.

As I stand mute, in shock, sickened, Dr. Mannis gently beats his chest and starts to chant, "Oh, God . . . Oh, God . . . Oh, God." He rocks back and forth, muttering ancient Hebraic words. He must reach out to the faith of his father to support the lack of faith he has in himself. This rebellious, arrogant, fire-eating liberal, who derisively cast off his background as one would an old coat, now instinctively slips it back on. It will be his armor against the unknown enemy.

Dr. Blakely, incredibly, unbelievably, is smiling. I have seen men smile in shock, in depair, in defeat, but his is one of triumph. Dr. Carlson has literally been torn apart, and Dr. Blakely is smiling. Am I mad at what I see and what I hear him saying? "Oh, yes, yes . . . Thank you, God."

2:15 A.M. . . . Through some inner source of willpower, I have forced myself to help Dr. Blakely cover the body with sheets, tuck the sheets under the body, scooping along as much of the entrails and organs as we can, and then carry the encased body out into the basement hallway.

The blood and other body matter that remain we simply cover with sheets.

We now have an answer. What it is or what it means we do not know, but it is an answer. Nothing remotely human killed Dr. Carlson. Whatever is beyond death came from that beyond to do it. It is something to be terrified of. It is with us.

Dr. Mannis informs Dr. Warner of what has happened. His answer, rather than shocked, is shocking. "Then we were right. There *is* something. It is not the end. I am merely waiting."

It is almost an exultant statement. Then my rational mind tells me, why should he be shocked? He is dead—who knows where—and we have informed him of a supernatural happening. Why shouldn't he feel exultant? Why should he feel sorrow? Haven't we just told him that he does not face oblivion, that no matter how harrowing the future, how bizarre eternity may be, haven't we affirmed there is one?

We have triumphed. We *were* right all the time. Death is not the end, just the beginning . . . but the beginning of what? Our triumph is a fearful one. Just what have we triumphed over, and is it really a victory? Knowledge may not necessarily mean power.

Dr. Mannis is composed, contemplative. Dr. Blakely is almost ecstatic. He has already relegated Dr. Carlson's death to a laboratory risk. He was right not to let Dr. Warner cut off. He cares not what the results may be, just so results are obtained, theories proved.

SIMON'S SOUL

Dr. Warner's thoughts are fed out of the computer to us. He asks for details of Dr. Carlson's death. As best we can remember, without going out to uncover the body, we relate what we saw. His answer is chilling. "It was done by whatever is beating on the dark curtain."

"Why?"

"It wants me, and you have stopped it."

Then I have been correct all along. *We* are the dark curtain that separates him from the beyond. By holding on to his mind, we have held on to his soul or spirit and kept it from taking the next step, whatever that next step is. "We should have let him go. Dr. Carlson would still be alive."

Dr. Blakely has recovered his composure and his caustic control. "But then we never would have known what we know, would we?" he asks. "Dr. Carlson is a fallen soldier. But then soldiers are supposed to fall, aren't they? The remainder of the army marches on, doesn't it?" Dr. Blakely smiles a cold smile that matches the temperature of his gray eyes. He is aroused by the impending battle. "It wants Simon badly. Whatever in eternity's name it is, it wants him badly enough to come to us."

"Why would it kill Leonard?"

"As a warning to free Simon."

"Why couldn't it free Simon itself?" Dr. Mannis asks. "If it could destroy Leonard, why couldn't it destroy the machines that are keeping Simon alive?"

I do not wish to side with Dr. Blakely at this moment, but my instincts tell me he is more right than wrong. "Perhaps it can destroy only flesh and blood, spirit and soul, or whatever man is made of. It might be helpless

Stanley Shapiro

against what man has made." Another instinct flutters into distant view, quite small but nevertheless there. "Perhaps there are rules that the Hereafter itself has to abide by. Rules and regulations and tradition."

"Which we have broken," says Dr. Mannis. "I think we should end this." He stares at Dr. Blakely. "Leonard's death is as far as I want to go."

"Out of friendship or fear?" Dr. Blakely replies. "The supernatural. Isn't that why we are all here to begin with? We have just opened the first door."

Have we indeed opened a door, formerly forever closed, with life on one side and the Hereafter on the other. Will it enable us to go in or permit something to rush out?

"We must go on." Dr. Blakely states a simple fact.

"But Leonard is dead, and it is our fault," Dr. Mannis protests.

"And Simon is dead, and that is also our fault," Dr. Blakely counters. "Don't be so despondent, Dr. Mannis. Death is not the end. We've just proven that."

2:55 A.M. ... We have neglected the messages coming from Dr. Warner. There is an almost constant transmission.

"The pressure against the curtain is stronger ... as if the curtain is thinner."

Thinner? Can Dr. Carlson's death have diminished its thickness? If we *are* the curtain, then our death will eliminate it.

"Do you want it to get to you, Simon?"

"Yes."

If we let him go, what is it he will go to? To this

SIMON'S SOUL

hideous force that murdered Dr. Carlson? Is that what is beyond death, horror? Surely whatever did this to Dr. Carlson cannot represent God. Of can it? But God is good. Or is He?

"Simon, do you feel any other presence out there? One that is comforting or gentle or peaceful?"

"None."

Dr. Blakely speaks into the tape recorders that are constantly running to record our voices. "We know that forces exist beyond human sight, sound, or normal comprehension. Whether we have souls or spirits is still to be determined."

"Aren't the facts proof enough?" Dr. Mannis asks.

"Not yet." Blakely wants hard, firm, undeniable proof. "What may exist may be other worlds that coexist with ours, which we call spirits or demons. That doesn't make it part of the Hereafter. Or it may be life from other galaxies. We must leave that option open. We haven't proved we have souls, just that there are other forces not normally seen or felt."

We pose this hypothesis to Dr. Warner.

"No, I do not agree," he answers. "If they are forces from coexisting worlds on different planes or from other planets, why should we have come in touch with them at this precise moment? Why would my death cause their appearance? I believe the force we have encountered is directly tied to us in a life-death-afterlife cord."

"Is it an evil force, Simon?"

There is a hesitation, and his answer comes back, practical, logical, suggesting a theory we have forgotten to think of. "Perhaps I have already been judged and been found unfit for Heaven. Perhaps it is an emissary from Hell who has come to get me."

Hell. Messengers from Satan who have come to claim a soul that is now rightfully theirs. Staggering. But with a dead man lying on the table, another out in the basement hall, those of us remaining will not declare anything impossible or improbable.

And then it happens.

The room is filled with a horrifying, hideous, ear-shattering scream.

We turn our heads to look, and it is there.

FIVE

A demon, an evil spirit, whatever it is, it stands in the room. About seven feet in height—semitransparent—its head and body covered with blood and boils and running sores—jagged scars from which wisps of dirty gray smoke come out—for eyes and mouth just burning black holes from which bright red molten fire oozes. It holds up what is an arm, with hundreds of tiny holes, from which worms and maggots crawl—and at the end of the arm, not fingers but a jagged claw dripping with blood—the claw that ripped Dr. Carlson apart. It points the claw at Dr. Warner, then at itself, shrieks a thousand terrors, and disappears.

The shock of the sight, the paralyzing effect of the sound, the insane laugh reverberating in our skulls. Evil-force waves pound the room, bounce off the walls, and engulf us over and over again, until the screams we hear are our own. We are standing there screaming in terror, in hysterical reaction to this monstrous nightmare. We are holding our hands to our ears, shrieking in fear, trying to survive this awful moment by nearly going insane.

Little by little, our screams become loud yells, then moans, then exhausted, heavy gasps for air. Dr. Mannis falls heavily to the floor. Dr. Blakely and I look at each other. We know what we have seen. We will not talk about it.

Dr. Mannis is dead. His heart cannot carry the burden of his eyes and ears.

3:10 A.M. ... Dr. Blakely and I, making many useless, unnecessary, blundering moves, have somehow dragged Dr. Mannis' body to a corner. I remove my jacket and cover his face with it. I do not try to close his eyes, nor do I look into them. I am afraid to see what his pupils will reflect.

Awkwardly working the computer, we manage to relay to Dr. Warner what has occurred. The coldness of his answer jars us back into a near-normal reality. "Fascinating. Soon we will know. We will know."

I have to force myself to accept that what are unspeakable horrors to us are comforting facts to him. How can a dead man become emotional about another man dying? I stare at this lifeless body packed in ice. Suddenly he is no longer a colleague I am working with. He is not the subject of a study. He is a mysterious, frightening entity. A dead body with a mind. A mind harboring a soul that is wanted by a fearsome force. Dr. Warner is no longer a human I once knew but a thing I am beginning to fear. No longer a partner but a potential peril.

"It's over. It's over!" I yell. "Let whatever it is have him!"

"No! Not over! Beginning! Just beginning!" Dr. Blakely is shouting back at me. Some inner spirit is rallying him against the trauma of the terror he has experienced. "We are close . . . so very close."

"To what? Death?" I shout back.

"Birth, afterbirth. Life, afterlife. Death, afterdeath."

I do not understand his words, only my fears. "It's over. Done."

"Not done. Not done. We have a right to know. To know all. Who we are. Why we are here. Where we are going. Man has a right to know everything."

"It might be against God's wishes."

"Where is He, Doctor? Where is God? We're created in His image. Was that His image we just saw?" Dr. Blakely starts to walk around the room, looking skyward, yelling in anger, in frustration, "Where are you, God? We've seen death and demons. Where is life and love? We believe in you. We're trying to find Heaven. Where are you?" He is shouting louder now. "Where are you, God? Who are you? Why are you? Was that you we saw just now?"

I scream at Dr. Blakely, "That was not God! Not God!"

We stand in the room, he on one side of Dr. Warner's body, I on the other side of it, yelling at each other at the top of our voices.

"It was not God, not God! God is beautiful!"

"Maybe that's what beauty truly is."

"God is Heaven."

"Maybe He's Hell."

"I love God! I love Him!"

"You'll pray to what you saw."

I sink to my knees, my head against the table Dr.

Warner's body lies on. Sobbing, I repeat over and over childhood phrases that must sustain me now. "God is good, God is mercy, God is love, God is today, God is forever."

Dr. Blakely and I are quiet, exhausted. We have relieved our shocked systems through our outburst. Our adrenaline has countered the trauma. Surviving has given us a momentary serenity. We discuss this incredible situation with a calmness we might use in talking about minor surgery.

"It pointed to Simon and then to itself," I analyze, "as if to say, 'He belongs to me.'"

Dr. Blakely nods his head. "It doesn't want to kill us. I mean, not all of us. If we all die, it may never get Simon's soul, if that is what it's after. Whatever its powers, it cannot shut off the machine. It needs human hands to do that."

"Why didn't it just kill us and wait?" I ask, trying to reason it out. "Surely it knows that eventually the machine has to be turned off, either by malfunction, by mistake, by us or by others."

It must know that eventually Dr. Warner's soul will belong to it. Again, previous instincts lead to new instincts. "Maybe it can't wait for it to happen. Maybe eternity has a schedule it must adhere to. Maybe it must take the soul within a certain period or else lose it."

Dr. Blakely will accept any thesis that will continue the experiment. "We'll proceed on that basis, Ben. That it wants Simon's soul. That time is short, and it is now desperate."

SIMON'S SOUL

Demons, souls, Hell. Wild, mad speculation. I apologize for none of it. Not after what I have seen.

"I think," says Dr. Blakely, "I think it will kill one more of us, and hope the survivor will turn off the machine."

There is a calculated calm about him. No longer brisk, brutal. The terror he has seen has left a residue of almost beatific balm on his normally biting, baiting tongue. One of us will die. He will take that half chance that it won't be he. That this thing, with only him remaining, desperately needing him to turn the machine off, will reveal immortal, eternal, hidden secrets in exchange for his doing so. He is willing to face it to fathom it. He is a braver man than I.

"I'm sorry I spoke ill of God," he apologizes. I just nod my head. "I hold no grudge if God doesn't."

I speak softly, hoping softness will not agitate him. "Let him go, Stuart. Let him go."

"No, Ben. Not without finding out what it is."

"It's Hell."

"Then I want Hell's secrets."

I now remember where I have seen that serene look before: on the face of a researcher who was working on bacteria that could wipe out the human race ... in the eyes of a physicist who was refining the hydrogen bomb. There is a dedication to death that obliterates fear of death. Dr. Blakely has survived the worst. Now he wants to calmly dissect the worst to learn its secrets.

My only hope is Dr. Warner. We explain the situation as we have seen it and feel it to be. His answer is brisk,

Stanley Shapiro

imperative. "Yes, let me go. Let me go immediately. . . . It has come for me. . . . I must go."

We are suddenly no longer communicating with an objective, rational, analytical mind. It is one filled with an explosive urgency, begging to be released to this unearthly, fiendish nightmare.

"Go where, Simon, where?" Dr. Blakely forces the issue.

"I don't know. . . . I must go. . . . It can't leave without me. . . . I must become part of it. . . . or it will become part of me. . . . part of my body."

"Your body is dead, Simon."

"It will enter. . . . Once it enters it can never leave."

"Never leave what, Simon?"

"Your earth. In his name, let me go."

"Let him go, Stuart."

"No." With a sweep of his muscular arm, he sends me stumbling across the room. He feeds questions into the computer. "In *his* name? In *whose* name?"

"I'm not sure."

"Say God almighty, Simon."

"I can't."

"Say Jesus Christ."

"I can't."

"Say Satan."

"Satan, Satan, beloved Satan. Teacher. Master. It's coming. . . . Let me go. . . . It's coming."

Dr. Blakely triumphantly stands between me and the machines. "They were right. Our father's fathers were right. We have souls. There *is* a Heaven and a Hell. No matter how dreadful, it's beautiful. There is peace and punishment, rest and reward. There is a plan, a procedure. We've upset it. It has to reveal itself."

"The machine. Damn it, turn it off." I lunge for it.

He grabs me. Strong by nature, stronger by the nature of his obsession. "No, we can't shut off eternity." His eyes now shine with the intensity of a man possessed, who is running toward a goal only *his* subconscious can see.

I try to pull free. "It will kill us."

"What is death?" he shouts. "It's not the end. It's only a first step. We challenged it and won. We don't die, Ben. Threaten me with life, not death."

"We're upsetting the balance."

"What balance?"

"I don't know." And I didn't. It's a phrase that had suddenly entered my mind. "It belongs there, and we belong here."

"No. Man belongs wherever he can learn. To settle for less is to lose superiority."

The temperature in the room is dropping sharply. A chill is filling it, like ice water being poured into a bowl.

"We are not superior," I cry, "not superior. . . . and it's coming."

His answer is that of a superior. "We made it come to us. We'll make it bend to us." His eyes are protected from reality by a deep, self-hypnotic glow. Somewhere in the past minutes of the past events he has become insane. "Why does Simon want us to leave him?" he confides, holding my arm in a madman's grip. "Because he wants all the credit for discovering eternity. Don't you see, Ben," he says with a sly, knowing smile, "he doesn't need us anymore. We are a burden, partners he no longer wants."

The room is at near-zero temperature. I am trembling with cold and with fear. Dr. Blakely, incredibly, is perspiring. His adrenal flow is so intense, his emotional pitch so high, that his nervous system is no longer reacting to external facts but to internal fantasies.

He may kill me, but I must make one desperate leap toward the body, tear the electrodes from the skull, rip out the tubes that supply the brain with oxygen and blood.

The room is again filled with that hideous, mind-shattering shriek. I look, but I do not see anything. That hellish howl is coming from Dr. Warner. The dreadful sound is passing through his lips like a malignant hurricane. And then Dr. Warner's arm begins to move.

SIX

Dr. Warner is lifting his arm. He removes the needles and tubes from the arteries through which they have been pumping oxygen and blood. He pulls the electrodes from his skull. He pushes aside the rubber sacks containing the ice that has been cooling his body against deterioration. He slowly sits up on the operating table, looks at us through dead eyes, and again emits that terrifying shriek.

It is in his body. This malevolent spirit or demon is within him. This unholy, evil energy has slipped on his rotting earthly garment. It has come for Dr. Warner's soul. It has it, but it too is now a prisoner. The soul and this monstrous soul-seeker now share this dead dungeon.

Dr. Blakely laughs victoriously, irrationally unaware of the catastrophe. "We've got it. We've trapped it." The sight of a dead body laboriously getting off the operating table and approaching him produces a feeling of triumph, not terror. He points at it as it step by step, as though it is learning to walk, heads toward him. "You wanted the glory for yourself, Simon. You would deny us knowledge and honor. You would have left us in our mortal ignorance. We will hold you to your earthly vestments. The evil you've done does not live after you. It lives with you."

Dr. Warner's mouth opens, and from it comes a rasping, grating roar, a mixture of sounds unknown to earth, filled with a hate and an anger unknown to earth.

Dr. Blakely laughs, insanely unaware. Spittle runs down his chin; he is filled with some mad, inner mirth. "We've trapped it, Simon. You will help us examine it, learn its secrets, and we will all equally share in the glory."

Again that awful roar from Dr. Warner's mouth, as though a thousand dying animals were crying out in pain.

Dr. Warner's eyes start to open and close. Whatever is inside him is experimenting with his eyes. They have a look that goes beyond malice or anger. The eyes are the core of pure, absolute, final evil.

Dr. Blakely is laughing uncontrollably. "And just what have we caught in this simple human trap? We shall look you over very carefully indeed, my inhuman friend."

Dr. Warner's hand slashes at Dr. Blakely, wickedly but awkwardly. Dr. Blakely dodges it. As Dr. Blakely backs away, he derides it. "You're still awkward, my friend. You haven't learned how to move that body yet, have you?" With a smile, he faces the oncoming Dr. Warner but talks to me. "Observe, Benjamin, limitless, infinite energy trapped in a limited, finite body."

SIMON'S SOUL

With another horrific roar from another unknown world, Dr. Warner swings at Dr. Blakely again, misses, falls against a table containing surgical equipment. A scalpel embeds itself deep in his stomach. He takes it out of his stomach, stares at it. Its cutting edge has no effect on his dead flesh.

Dr. Warner gropes along the floor, pushes himself to his feet. He looks at the large glass cylinder into which we have drained the pints of his lifeblood. He picks it up, holds it high above his head, stumbles toward Dr. Blakely, who laughs and dances away, so that Dr. Warner has to keep turning to keep him in sight. With a searing scream, he heaves the cylinder of blood at Dr. Blakely, who dodges it, and it smashes against the wall, exploding blood all over the room.

Dr. Blakely cries out in vindication. "We *are* superior. Look at him. This Hell creation, capable of cosmic chaos, limited only to the evil the human body is capable of." As he backs away from the approaching hatred, he is planning the future. "We will cage him, study him, talk to him. The price of his freedom, if free he can ever be again, will be knowledge. He will tell us about the beginning and the end, the universe and beyond the universe. We *are* superior. We *will* conquer Heaven and Hell."

Moving backward, Dr. Blakely slips on the bloodied floor. His hands slide on slick blood as he tries to get up. Dr. Warner is upon him.

A mad Dr. Blakely and a dead Dr. Warner roll in the

red liquid that is garnished with a thousand bits of splintered glass. Hands reach for the other's throat. One possessed by madness, the other by an infinitely stronger power. It has made Dr. Warner's fingers close on Dr. Blakely's throat with a grip so savage, so intense, that it is almost more than the hand can tolerate without its own bones breaking. Dr. Blakely's neck is snapped; his eyes bulge and start to ooze out of their sockets. He is a dead man before he can fully comprehend it.

Dr. Warner drops Dr. Blakely's body, rises, turns, and starts toward me.

I have been rooted to the floor like a tree to the ground. Now his eyes turn to mine. What image is flashed to whatever is now within him? What is it that is looking out through those sightless pupils? How can it move a body that has no blood, no nerves, no living cells or flesh? Why can't I, a living being, order *my* body to move, to run, to flee?

Dr. Warner points a finger at me, and from his mouth comes the first word. Dead vocal cords form the word. Whatever it is within him pushes the word out, a deep, bass monotone that is being slid across thick sandpaper. "Die."

What movements could not do, that human word does. My uncomprehending, hypnotic fascination turns to a comprehending, terrorized fear. I twist around and force myself toward the door. I grasp the knob and try to turn it, but can't. He is coming closer. Is it stuck? Am I too weak with fear? I start to cry as my sweating hands slip on the bright metal. He is almost upon me. It opens.

SIMON'S SOUL

I am out the door and close it behind me. I hear his hands beat on the door and then grasp the knob to turn it. I cannot hold it against his strength. The basement corridor is perhaps thirty-five feet in length and leads to the stairway. Up the stairway is the basement door, which leads to the house. If I can get to the stairway, up it, and through the door, I can bolt it from the outside. It has a heavy metal bolt. If I can just get to the stairs. I start to run. The door behind me opens, and he is coming after me, down the narrow corridor, with his stumbling, lumbering gait. The stairs seem so far away. . . . I seem to be moving in slow motion, one gliding step after the other. . . . It is like a childhood nightmare, where you try to run as you are pursued by some ghoulish presence, but you cannot move fast enough. Each step is a slow, labored, torturous effort . . . except now it is a real nightmare.

I start up the stairs. He has reached the foot of them, and lunges at me. His hand just touches the heel of my shoe. He falls, gets to his knees, and starts to drag himself up. . . . Oh, God, please, let me be able to open that door. I grasp the handle, turn it, push. It holds firm. . . . I am dead in another moment. . . . Please, God, open it. . . . I push and it opens. I fall through, grab the handle on the other side, slam it shut, and slide the heavy bolt into place. Just in time, barely in time. As the bolt slides shut, his body hurls itself against the door.

I sink to the floor in exhaustion. The effort has drained me of even the strength to stand. It continues to throw its body against the door, beating on it, uttering unintelligible, obscene cries. But it cannot break down the thick door. Dr. Blakely was correct. Its outrage is that its frightening force is now contained in a human body and limited to the powers of flesh and bone.

I am in the entry hall that leads to the basement. The screaming and pounding from behind the door continue. I crawl across the floor, then turn, and, sitting on the floor, look and listen as the door quivers under this thing's frantic efforts, but it holds. It is the only way out of the basement. Dr. Blakely wanted to cage it. I have caged it. But what have I caught? Whom do I tell? Who will believe me? Of course they'll believe me. Maybe not before, when all we had was a corpse and messages that were supposed to be coming from it. But now they will have this thing behind that door. It exists. Let them examine it. A body without blood, without a heartbeat, without living cells. Let that indescribable inhumanity within him shriek its terrifying sounds. They will believe.

It is quiet on the other side of the door. I pick up the telephone. Whom should I call? Why don't my thoughts go to my wife, the police, other doctors? Instead I want to phone some unknown person, some all-knowing being, who will understand all in a moment. Who will take this terrible experience off my shoulders into his capable hands. That person does not exist. No one can carry the burden of explanation but myself.

There is the sudden sound of metal slamming into heavy wood. What is it doing? The door shakes violently under the blows. Somewhere in that basement it has found an ax.

I ask the operator for the police as the door slowly,

SIMON'S SOUL

grudgingly, starts to give way. A human voice answers. "Police Department. Sergeant Toomlin."

I yell it out all at once, releasing everything in a jumble of words. "Ninety-two ninety-seven Cerino Drive—please come—quickly or it's too late." Words pour out, unconnected, unrelated, panicked words. "It's not human—it wants to kill—they're all dead—except me—in God's name, please come—Ninety-two ninety-seven Cerino Drive—it's trying to get out the door—please come."

The bolt is snapped free from its moorings. The door swings open. Dr. Warner stands there, ax in hand. The shriek of hate engulfs me in gross decibels. Has that police sergeant at the other end heard it? I drop the phone, roll over onto my side, push myself to my feet, and start to run. Dr. Warner throws the ax at me. It flies wildly over my head and embeds itself in a painting on the wall.

Through the living room, tripping, falling, rising, running. It crosses the living room after me, falling over a chair, a table, as though it does not see too well yet with these new eyes. It has not learned to work the body yet. It gets up, smashes the offending furniture with its hand, and, staggering, propels the body after me.

Out the front door into the night. This lonely house in this deserted mountain area. In the best of times a solitary, desolate place, it now becomes a sightless ally of the terror that is chasing me. It is like the dark curtain that Dr. Warner was once surrounded by. I am afraid to run into it, for in its darkness I will be lost, trapped, caught. I will stumble, twist, turn, and recross my path,

Stanley Shapiro

and I will run into its waiting, murderous arms. The night is not the friend of fearful flight.

But beyond the dark curtain is something, a pulse beat I am familiar with, life as I know it, not as I have found it here. Beyond the darkness are people like myself. I must reach them.

I run into the night, across the graveled courtyard. I stop to listen. I hear the slow, measured steps crushing the gravel behind me. I turn and run into it. I start to scream and beat on it until I realize I am smashing my hands on metal, on a parked car. One of the cars we had parked in the driveway of the courtyard. I had forgotten about the cars left in the driveway. Driven into a world I had never imagined possible, I had forgotten about the world I had driven out of and what had brought me here.

I reach into my pocket. They're there! My car keys! I open the door, plunge in, slam the door behind me. Quickly, quickly, it must be done quickly. Desperate fingers find the ignition slot, push the key in. It won't fit. It doesn't fit. It's not my car.

The gravel gives way near me. It is outside the door. As it opens the door, I hurl myself across to the other door, reach for the handle, cannot find it. Please, let me open the door. I don't want to die in this car. Sweating hands find the handle, push. The door opens and I throw myself onto the ground outside. As I fall, I hear its hand come down hard on the empty seat where I had just been. I hear the piercing cry of anger that I am not there.

I scramble across the tiny cutting stones, on my hands and knees, leaving pieces of skin and clothing to mark my

SIMON'S SOUL

trail. My hands touch a rubber tire. I reach up, grasp a door handle, and lift myself. I anxiously run my hands over the metal body as one would over a long-lost lover. Is it mine or just a silent steel widow of one of the dead men? I am betrayed by the canvas of its convertible top.

The sound of an engine turning over. It has found a car with keys in it. Headlights go on. Light. Light that I so desperately wanted has been turned against me. Two accusing, burning fingers point at me. I see my car beyond the one I am standing against.

Its foot has come down so forcefully on the accelerator, its anger is infused into the machine. Frenzied wheels spin so fast, the car is frozen in place. Then wheels and ground become one and it leaps forward, hurtling toward me.

I throw myself through the air as it smashes into the side of the car where I had stood a microsecond before. Dr. Warner's body is hurled forward by the impact of the crash. His head goes through the front window, and is pulled back. A jagged piece of glass sticks from the throat. There is no blood, no injury, no shock. The car starts to back away, pulling the other car with it where twisted metal has locked with twisted metal.

He backs up, drives forward, and backs up again, trying to free the car. In the shadows of the car's muted headlights, it is a bizarre scene, like an angry bull trying to shake loose its rider.

I run to my car. The door is locked. As I frantically try to feel the door key in the tangle of keys I hold, I curse myself for locking doors.

It has pulled free from its metal tormentor by sacrificing a bumper.

I have the door open, get in, search for the ignition.

One of its headlights has gone out. It is left with one probing, silvery eye.

I've pushed the key into the ignition and turned. The motor, which has served me faithfully, must serve me this one final time. "Start, start, you son of a bitch. You stupid bastard, start." I am yelling at it, cursing it, begging it.

The single headlight finds and holds me, like a hunting dog pointing out the prey.

The key will turn no farther without snapping. The motor grinds, grinds, grinds, and turns over. Oh, beautiful for spacious Ford, God shed His light on thee.... The one-eyed death bird is bearing down on me. I go into reverse gear, back off, and it brushes past me and smashes into another parked car. I switch the headlights on. The gate—where is the gate out of this holocaust? I see it at the same time it has backed free. I gun the car toward freedom. It heads for my freedom to cut me off. It is not a mile race where you can plan strategy. It is a short dash where you expend all energy in one furious burst of power.

A ten-foot-wide escape hatch, on each side a steel fence. In those fifty yards my fifty years will be forfeit. I am at the gate, through it. Roaring down at me from the side, it is just part of a hair too late. It brushes my rear fender, goes crashing and sliding along the iron fence.

I am on the road, wildly careening along the snakelike mountaintop, going fast, far too fast, along the sharp

SIMON'S SOUL

curves. I turn right and start down the winding road, skidding, braking, pressing the accelerator again. In the rearview mirror I see the single headlight. One moment it is on the road, the next, it has gone over the mountainside, for the headlight suddenly turns itself toward the heavens, as though trying to expose the road that leads to the universe. Then it begins to turn slowly in an arc and fall, fall, fall, like a shooting star. The light goes dark forever, out forever, as the car plunges into the mountain bottom, and seconds later another light replaces it, the light of the exploding gas tank, and then the raging fire as heat tries to consume steel.

I brake the car and sit, silently staring at the tiny lights of Los Angeles below. To a microscopic creature they would be the stars of a distant galaxy, with unseen, unknown secrets behind them. To me, behind those lights are humans like myself. Knowledge is many times a matter of distance. If we can reach out and touch, we are aware. We reached out, beyond death, and touched a gruesome vision, an awesome, fearsome force. Is the satisfaction of knowing there is something beyond death worth knowing what it is?

I still do not know what it is, but I know it is still with us. If I could do it over, I would opt for the rector over the researcher, the sermon over science.

Does knowing there is something beyond death change death or life? Wasn't believing enough? Have we changed natural and unnatural laws? A natural man is dead, and an unnatural force is within him. Can it go back from whence it came? Can it return with the soul it came to take, or is this poisonous power and the soul it came for locked forever in that rotting carcass?

We have seen Hell's emissary. As foul as it is, I must imagine Heaven's ambassador is fair, fairer than our purest prayer. Or is it from just another spiritual level? Is it just another step, and then there will be another death, another life after, and on and on? Are there many eternities, each with its rules and regulations? Life may be but a transition point, from whence to where I do not know, or how many whences and how many wheres.

Now that I have seen, I understand why they say, "May his soul rest in peace." Oh, the respect I have for our ancient ancestors. They understood. The past was wiser than the present, for they understood the future.

SEVEN

"Are you all right?" I hear it faintly. In repetition it becomes clearer. I raise my head from against the car wheel I have been leaning on, blowing a steady sound on the horn. I remember where I am, but how long have I been here? Police cars parked on the winding road, fire trucks, huge floodlights lighting up the valley below where the car crashed. Men are lowering themselves down the mountainside by ropes.

"Are you all right?" he asks as he looks at me. I see the obvious conclusion on his face. A battered car and driver, either drunk or high on drugs, in an accident with another car, forcing it off the road over the cliff.

I open the door and half stagger, half run to the small wood guard rails by the edge of the road. I point toward the smoking ruins below. "Don't let it get away. It can't be killed. Don't let it get away."

The officer's arm holds mine firmly. "Easy, mister, there's no one can get away from what's down there."

Stanley Shapiro

I pull my arm free, grab his, and shout urgently, "Yes, yes, it can. You've got to believe me. It can't be killed. He's already dead." I cannot stop myself from trying to explain. "If you see him, bind him in chains, put him in a cell. It's limited by the body it's in."

Other officers come to assist him. My arms are moved behind my back; the steel handcuffs bruise my wrist bones. "You don't understand. I'm a doctor. It was an experiment. It's already killed three of us."

As I am guided and pushed into a police car, a distant voice shouts the news. "It's weird down there. They say they can't find anyone in the car."

August 30 . . .

Whether I have slept out of fatigue, hysteria, relief, or as an escape, I am now in a hospital bed, the restraining strap across my chest. The psychiatric ward at County Hospital. I have been here before but not as a patient. My wife and son stand there, looking down at me. I feel concern in my wife's face, a sort of distant look of interest in my son's countenance. Behind them stands a friend of many years, Dr. Leslie Rettenmund, a psychiatrist, and Arnold Hansen, my attorney.

"Are you all right, Ben?" my wife asks.

"No, I am not all right." I am perfectly frank.

My son says, "You're charged with a triple slaying and one disappearance."

I look at his uninvolved face. "Thanks, son, I needed that."

"We know you didn't do it." My wife consoles me.

"Did you, Dad?" my son asks, almost hopefully. He will

SIMON'S SOUL

be a big hero among his peers. How many kids have fathers who have committed multiple murders?

I shake my head no. My wife puts her head in her hands and cries. "Oh, thank God. Thank God." If she is that relieved, was she really so sure I didn't do it when she said she knew I didn't do it? It doesn't matter.

I look toward Dr. Rettenmund. "Did he get away?"

"Who, Ben?"

"Dr. Warner."

"Away from where, Ben?"

"The car. The car that crashed."

"No one was in that car, Ben. No one could have been in that car and lived, much less left."

How can I tell them that Dr. Warner was already dead when it crashed? That this thing is inside him, controlling the dead body. Where is it now? Is it trying to find me? Does it have to find me in order to carry out some supernaturally ordained revenge?

"They say it's the worst thing since the Manson family, Dad, except you didn't need a family."

I look at my son. Indeed I don't need a family. I want to thank him sarcastically for that useful bit of information. "I hope it's some kind of record. I've always wanted to be in the *Guinness Book of World Records.*" I turn to Dr. Rettenmund. "Tell them to go back to the basement. There's a computer. It monitored our conversations. There are records of every message we sent him and everything Dr. Warner thought back."

"Everything Dr. Warner thought?"

"He was dead, Leslie. I'll explain later."

An hour later, Dr. Rettenmund comes back with the first ill omen. More than ill, ominous. No recorded tapes of any conversations were found in the computer.

They're gone. It is thinking, planning. It got out of the car, found its way back to the house, destroyed the tapes. It doesn't want us to find them. The less the world knows about it, the better. Let me be the only spokesman for its existence. Let a suspected madman convince the world of the truth.

"Arnold, I want to make a statement. I want you here as my lawyer, Leslie here as a psychiatrist, and I want three men of the cloth, a minister, a priest, and a rabbi. They must take an oath first that they believe in God, in Heaven and Hell, and in whatever impossibilities are possible in those places."

I hate the smile on my son's face. He is already making up the stories he will tell about his mad dad.

"Would you rather tell Leslie and me first?" Arnold asks.

"No. I saw it once. I can tell it only once."

August 31 . . .

I am still in the observation room, but for the occasion the leather restraints have been removed and I am allowed to sit in a straight-backed chair facing the men I have asked for. Arnold, my attorney, and Dr. Rettenmund, a psychiatrist, are both calm, competent men who may not panic when they hear my explanation. I am not sure about the holy men.

The Reverend Chisholm is a sleepy-eyed, overweight man, with what may be a smile or a smirk. Whereas

SIMON'S SOUL

sleepy eyes can be erotic in a woman, they can be erratic in a man.

Father Ryan is the old Irish priest we have seen in a thousand old movies. Sure and begorra, he believes in God. A God who loves the poor and wins football games for you. Will this wisp of a priest understand a God who may not be an Irishman?

Rabbi Holzman is a middle-aged man with an old man's philosophy. Prematurely bald, prematurely carrying the weight of men's sins on his shoulders, ready to answer a question with a question, to complicate it with an anecdote, and finally leave you with a conundrum. An intellectual who believes in God, which is why the Old Testament is part faith, part history. How will his intellect cope with something that is mind blowing?

I wanted holy men, I have been given stereotypes. Or are they one and the same thing?

Arnold has turned on a recorder, the information will later be typed up. I look at them all one last time before making my statement. Noncommittal, waiting faces. My peers, about to hear an unpeerlike tale. I must take my chance that the incredible will be accepted by skeptical men.

"Gentlemen, what I am about to tell you is truth. Think before you disbelieve. Ponder before you call it preposterous. Try to imagine it as a true happening, not as insanity. Pause and ask, 'Could this occur if there truly is something beyond death?'"

They stand, five pillars of logic, about to be assaulted.

"I have always believed in God, without asking for

Stanley Shapiro

proof. I never wondered if we are God's creation or if He is ours. God and the Hereafter existed for me and for the others. But no matter how firm the house of faith, occasionally a shadow of doubt passes over it. When you see life and all its visible manifestations, and then death and all its invisible myths, you want desperately to prove belief is not an illusion.

"If there's a soul, then the moment of death may be its transition point, and who is closer to the moment of death than doctors? If we just knew, at death's instant, what was happening. If the dead man could but tell us."

I see the look of concern pass over all their faces, except the Reverend Chisholm's. He retains that sleepy-eyed smile. I know I have lost him. He believes in miracle healing but not by physicians.

I recount, moment for moment, what had happened. Dr. Warner volunteering—decoding thought waves into words—feeding them into Dr. Warner—getting linguistic fingerprints—the oxygen and blood keeping his brain alive—his physical death—the dark curtain—the movement beyond it—Dr. Carlson's death—the shriek as it appeared.

As I come to that, to the old priest's credit, he crosses himself, as does Dr. Rettenmund. The rabbi sits down on a chair and rests his head in his hands.

I tell of the death of Dr. Mannis—of this thing entering Dr. Warner's dead body. The priest crosses himself again. How Dr. Blakely taunted it, teased it, triumphed over it, to the very moment of his own death. My flight—the terrifying chase—the car, with Dr. Warner's body driving it, plunging over the mountain. How it had gone back to the house to destroy the evidence—and at this moment was somewhere in the city—and my final plea, "Find him, examine him for the truth, then reexamine me for my sanity."

I turn off the recorder and stare at them. Only Dr. Rettenmund and the old priest look me in the eye, whether in disbelief or discovery I cannot tell.

The Reverend Chisholm's head has dropped to his chest in near sleep. He strokes the cross that hangs there, his earthly lullaby. Through almost closed eyelids he observes me, the smile never leaving his lips. He says nothing. He is trying to decide whether I am possessed or insane.

Arnold, who will defend me in court, takes refuge behind his own defenses, a legalese wall of impenetrable indecision. "I would like to study the transcript, Ben. It will give me a base to draw conclusions, not implications, either way." He doesn't believe me.

Dr. Rettenmund walks a fence for my benefit. "Interesting. Very interesting." Out of my sight, he will jump the fence but not to my side.

Rabbi Holzman continues to sit there, head in his hands. He speaks his words into his fingers. Not a statement but a question. "If I believe what is impossible about God, am I not disbelieving everything that is possible about God?" An incomprehensible question, which will puzzle the judge as well.

Father Ryan steps up to me, rests his hand on my shoulder. "Aye, I've heard a thousand confessions in my time. There is no man, sane or mad, sober or dirty drunk, who can make up a story like that." His hand squeezes my shoulder. "I believe every sacred, sinning word of it." I start to cry. I take his hand, put it to my eyes to catch the tears.

The others object. I am mad to my psychiatrist, guilty to my lawyer, possessed to the minister, a philosophy to the rabbi. But this little Irish priest, whose limits of credulity are associated with saints and elves and four-leaf clovers, who relies on the Pope to take care of the heavy stuff, *he* believes.

"And what's the man said?" he asks. "That there is a Hereafter. Am I to doubt that? That there is a judgment on whether it's Heaven or Hell with us. Am I to doubt that? That if the soul cannot go to the judgment, the judgment will come to it. Am I to doubt that? Am I to doubt that soul and judgment can be joined? That a hellish creature is in that body? Aye, half of Ireland's folktales are made of that mixture." And then his first gentle rebuke. "That they should not have tampered with the soul is not for me to say. But he has not tampered with the truth. Find Dr. Warner as he asks. Try the man for his blood, listen for his heart. We will know whether we've listened to a liar or a lunatic."

"I would suggest, Father," says the reverend, stifling a weary yawn, "that Dr. Warner's body is conveniently buried somewhere. That his car was pushed off the mountain."

Dr. Warner's body has to be found. If not, I will have to get a jury of twelve Irish priests.

EIGHT

The car ripped through the guard rail, turned in a slow, almost agonized somersault, came out of it grille first, and with thunderous impact met the mountain floor. Behind the wheel, it was aware of the body being thrust forward violently, the steering post entering just below the breastbone, the sharp snap-cracking of ribs, the louder, firmer breaking of a leg bone, the head being driven into the dashboard, opening a deep gash in the forehead, from which no blood flowed.

There was no fear to be felt, no pain to be endured, just a continuing, all-consuming feeling of anger and malice. An urge to kill, to destroy, ravage, and maim. To cut, slash, rip, and throttle. To kill and kill and kill again.

It made the body pull itself free of the steering post. It touched the hole beneath the breastbone out of curiosity, the broken ribs, one of which had penetrated a lung. It slid out through the opening left by a door that had been twisted off. It stood, realized it would have to wrap something around the broken leg bone to firm it so it could move on it. Not out of pain but out of the necessity that it had to mend this body in order to use it.

As it hobbled away, the flames burst from the car. In the orange-red glare, it viewed its surroundings. Trapped in this vulnerable body forever and ever. In ten times ten thousand years it could not exhaust the venomous rage and malice within it. It could only be vented and, at the same time, fed by destroying everything, every thing.

Return to the house, obliterate the machine that had recorded its capture. Tend the wounds so that the body was workable, not a broken toy whose clattering would attract attention. Change the outer garments called clothes. Master the body so it became a tool, not a burden. Caught, caged, consumed by endless, timeless furies. How to get back? How to get back?

September 2 . . .

My wife is at home, in shock. My son is at home, in vogue. He is surrounded by pimpled friends who glow in the grisly details. They sympathize as he shakes his head and says you spend a lifetime with a parent and never really know him. The dreams you have for mothers and fathers, and they turn out like this.

Father Ryan is allowed to visit me, accompanied by Deputy Inspector Wilson Flanagan, his sister's son. Inspector Flanagan is a practicing Catholic but also a practicing law-enforcement officer. Demons don't kill people. People kill people.

SIMON'S SOUL

"You'll have to excuse my nephew, Doctor," Father Ryan apologizes. "He believes in God so long as God stays where he belongs, in church. Christ will save us, but if he started to get off the cross, the Christians would start to flee."

Inspector Flanagan protests. "You're asking me to believe the impossible."

"Improbable I might accept," replies Father Ryan, "but not impossible. Impossible is the argument of the atheist."

"Of course there's a God," Flanagan says defensively.

"Find Dr. Warner, and you'll know it for sure," I say.

Flanagan eyes me accusingly. "A dead man walking around?" I nod my head, which turns accusation into anger. "Doctor, my uncle has spent fifty years serving God. He is going to retire next year. Let it be with honor, not humiliation. I want him mentioned for his service, not his senility."

Father Ryan fairly explodes. "Did you hear that? Senile, he's calling me. Seeing gray hairs where he should be seeing God. Senile, he says." He turns from appealing to me to lecturing his nephew. "I've not spent those fifty years looking down from papal heights, from the mountaintops of cardinals and bishops, viewing the struggling, praying masses below. I've been part of them, part of their struggle. I do not issue proclamations or policy. I hear confession and give consolation. Others may know what man should be. I only know what he is. I am not a scholar of creation but a student of the created. I know who prays and who preys. I have gotten these gray hairs being a human lie detector." He points his finger at me.

Stanley Shapiro

"And this man is telling God's truth as he saw it in Satan's demon."

Inspector Flanagan loves his uncle but is not lulled by him. "And when we find Dr. Warner, what do we charge him with, being dead? Harboring some spirit from another world? Do we give him a life sentence? After four hundred years does he get a parole?" Flanagan is perspiring. "If it's as you said, Doctor, I hope we never find him."

"His punishment isn't what we want," I say.

"What is it we want?"

"Confinement."

"For how long, Doctor? A hundred years? A thousand? Forever?"

"If need be, yes. Let one generation to the next be his keeper."

As he leaves, he says, "I don't know, maybe the Police Benevolent Association has a clause protecting me from all this."

"I don't blame him, Father."

"I do, Doctor. It's man's nature. He wants the convenience of religion without the consequences." He snaps his fingers. "Of course. Exorcism."

I shake my head negatively. "Exorcism is for removing an evil spirit from a living person. He's a dead man with something in him now that has his soul but cannot leave with it. Whatever it is cannot be exorcised or crucified or cursed or confessed away, only contained."

"If it were to get out of the body, what then?"

"I think it could destroy the world."

SIMON'S SOUL

"And it can't go back from where it came?"
"I don't think so. I'm not sure."
"Tell me, Doctor, why did you want to find the soul?"
"Because you kept telling us there is one."
"Couldn't you have believed us?"
"Have you believed it, Father? I mean at all times in your life, under all conditions? Absolutely believed without ever having had one tiny, minute doubt?"

He paused in honest thought. "Aye, I suppose we've all doubted. Even the saints themselves. It's a strange business, Doctor, this life and death."

It walked along the isolated mountain road. Its hate and raging pulses beat like a continuing savage storm against the body it was in.

The camper was parked off the road, near the edge of the precipice. It walked up and looked in through the partly drawn curtains that covered the window of the rear door. The woman, perhaps eighteen or nineteen years old, was in a sleeping bag.

It quietly opened the door and climbed in, went to its knees, with its left hand picked up a large nail that lay alongside some carpentry tools and with its right hand the hammer. It placed the point of the nail on her forehead, struck the head of the nail a thunderous blow with the hammer, driving the nail deep into her skull. It let out a shriek of hateful delight.

I am being examined by Doctors Roth and Harrison. They cannot shake my belief in what I saw. I am quite

Stanley Shapiro

calm. My effort not to convince them only supports their impression that I have convinced myself I actually saw what I claim. I am calm, not out of hopelessness but out of sadness. Soon its deeds will give credence to my story.

It steps out of the flower garden to the pool area. The small brown terrier comes running out the open kitchen door of the tree-secluded home. Barking furiously at the intruder, he leaps at him. It catches the dog by the throat, stifling the bark back down its throat, then lowers it into the pool.

It walks into the kitchen, through the living room, into the study. The man sits there, his back to it, cleaning a revolver. It picks up a poker iron, walks up behind the man, and brings iron down on skull, crushing it. It picks up the revolver. A box of target-practice bullets lies on the desk. It inserts the flat-nosed bullets into the gun, walks out of the study, past a bedroom, stops as it sees a child sitting, watching television. It walks up behind the child, points the gun, and fires. The maid comes running from an upstairs bedroom. She stares at it, at the child, screams. It points the gun at her and fires.

I do not understand why Father Ryan and Dr. Rettenmund sit so quietly as Inspector Flanagan and two other police officers question me. Their questions are no longer hostile. Their probing seems to be for information, not incrimination.

"This thing, whatever it is," says Flanagan, "if it exists, as you say, it wouldn't need food or drink."

SIMON'S SOUL

"No. Nor sleep nor rest."
"Where would it go? What would it do?"
"Kill."
"Kill what?"
"Everything it sees."
"Why?"
"It is absolute evil. That is the only way it can express its nature, by uncontrolled violence."
"For how long?"
"Forever. I don't know. I'm not sure."
"But so long as it is within Dr. Warner's body, its strength is confined to the body's strength?"
"I think so, yes."
"If you could, how would you go about finding him? I mean, obviously we will put out photos and descriptions of Dr. Warner. But aside from that?"
"By searching anywhere where senseless, violent murders have taken place."
They stand there studying me silently, thoughtfully.

It drives the bakery truck. The driver lies in the rear of the truck, the knife in his chest, his blood being absorbed by the loaves of bread he lies on.

The hitchhiker carries schoolbooks and a basketball uniform. It stops the truck.

"You going down to Sunset Boulevard?" the hitchhiker asks.

It makes Dr. Warner's head nod. The hitchhiker gets in the truck, closes the door after him. The truck starts down the hill again.

Stanley Shapiro

"Man, I was standing out there for half an hour. I figured I had to get lucky sometime," the hitchhiker says as he takes out a pack of cigarettes. "Want a smoke?"

It doesn't answer. The hitchhiker takes the silence for weariness. "Have a hard day, huh?" He lights the cigarette, tosses the match out the open window, turns, reacts to the gun pointing at him. He retains his cool. "Hey, man, you don't want me to smoke, I won't."

It fires the gun into the hitchhiker's face.

September 3 . . .

I am taken from the hospital to police headquarters. They are all there. Flanagan, other police, Father Ryan, the minister and the rabbi, the psychiatrists, my lawyer. Except for Father Ryan, who sits there, his head lowered, the others are pale, perspiring, extremely nervous. There is a large wall map of the city. I see the lines of red circles. I've been so busy defending my sanity I haven't had time to examine theirs. They are frightened men, not of me, of the red circles. What happened in those red circles? And I understand. I want to laugh in relief, curse them in anger, cry in sorrow. I try to make a trembling throat talk controlled words. "How many?"

Inspector Flanagan grimaces, then quietly says, "Six." He has to balance admission against lingering doubt. "There are lots of murders. . . . Crazy people everywhere . . . It could all be just a weird coincidence."

"Yes, that's possible," I admit. "Senseless murders happen every day. I mean it. I'm not trying to be facetious." I turn to the others. "What do you all think?"

SIMON'S SOUL

Dr. Roth says, "We must investigate, not jump to hasty conclusions that may embarrass us the rest of our lives."

The others nod in assent. He has taken the awful burden of giving an opinion off their not-too-sure shoulders.

Father Ryan gets to the bottom line. "How do we capture it, Doctor?"

"Tell me about the murders."

I am told. I walk over and study the street map with the red circles. I see the path they form, the direction they are heading. I cry out, "My house! It's going to my house!"

NINE

It drives the gray Cadillac down Holmby Avenue, alongside the university. It had simply stepped into the first car it had seen that had an ignition key in it.

Police cars, sirens wailing, race by. The Cadillac starts to lurch, its motor coughs, strongly at first, then weaker and weaker as the gas that feeds its steel organs runs thin, then runs out.

It steers the gliding car to a stop against the curb, gets out, and starts to walk across the campus.

My wife and son have been flown to San Francisco to stay with her parents. I am in my home with Inspector Flanagan, other police, and Father Ryan. I have asked for Father Ryan's presence. He understands. I feel comfortable with him.

I would feel more comfortable if I too could go to San Francisco, far enough away so that it couldn't reach me, so the trail of death it has left looking for me would serve

SIMON'S SOUL

as a warning to others, not to me. But it has forever to find me, and I do not have forever to run.

As it becomes more sophisticated about its body and its surroundings, it will take faster, cleverer steps to find me. It has to be found now, while it is still adjusting. It wants me. I am the last one who had brought it into the world who is still alive. The quickest way to find it is to let it feel it can find me. I will be the bait.

September 3 . . .

9:00 P.M. . . . I sit at the desk in my den, pretending to write. I know there are police nearby, but I feel very exposed, very vulnerable. They really do not know what it is they are stalking and what it is that is stalking me.

Is it forever trapped in Dr. Warner's body? It doesn't seem possible. Nothing that unknown, that ageless, that powerful, can forever remain prisoner in the known, the age-prone, the power limited.

It will find me. Let it do so now while it is containable, and pray it will take a thousand generations for it to break free.

Where is it now? Is it watching me? Will it be upon me before I can be helped?

The phone rings.

I pick it up, and the voice stifles the atmosphere, making it difficult to breathe. It has that bass, grating, sandpaper sound. The words are clear but come out one at a time like drops of acid. "Motherfucker . . . Cocksucker . . . Fucking . . . shit . . . Hate . . . hate . . . you . . . Kill . . . you . . . Tear . . . your . . . shitty . . . brains . . . out."

Stanley Shapiro

It hangs the phone up so violently it breaks off the hook that holds the receiver. Seething with violence, it jerks the phone-booth door open and smashes its fist into it, shattering the glass, opening large, bloodless cuts on its knuckles.

It walks along the confined concrete floor of the underground garage toward the ramp that leads to ground level. The swirling forces of destruction boil and overflow. It pounds on concrete pillars as it walks up the ramp.

The small Volkswagen comes around the curve of the ramp and hits it before brakes can be applied. Hits it and goes over it before the petrified woman driving the car can stop. She forces her way out of the car and runs toward the man lying there, screaming, "I'm sorry. I didn't see you. I didn't see you."

She kneels over the prone body, pleading, "Please, please don't die. Can you hear me?" It lets the roar out of its mouth, into her face and mind, scorching the face, crushing the mind. The hand reaches up and grabs her throat, squeezing its anger into her.

9:15 P.M. . . . That call has frightened me more than if it had come straight here. I tell Inspector Flanagan I'd rather have a mad bull charge me than one that is thinking, weighing its chances.

Father Ryan, bless him, bless him, the last one I would ever have expected to understand, understands all. "Don't judge the Irish by an Irish cop," he says. Before Inspector Flanagan can protest, Father Ryan explains. "Dr. Warner is part of this thing now, like part of a stew. He's given

SIMON'S SOUL

thought to what was thoughtless, reasoning power to what was unreasonable, information and direction to what was uninformed and aimless. It is starting to make use of the knowledge in the doctor's soul. How to drive, to make phone calls, to avoid while advancing. What would you rather be caught in, nephew, a mindless hurricane or one that planned what it would destroy?"

Inspector Flanagan is defensive. "Look, I'm only human. It took me years to learn to think like a criminal. I can't learn to think like an evil spirit overnight."

It is nearing the doctor's house. It can feel his presence. It bares Dr. Warner's teeth in an animal-like snarl. A rumbling, ominous moan comes from Dr. Warner's throat. Fists open and close in reflex action to the inner raging fires.

It is walking along the dark streets. Overhead it sees the police helicopters. They swing in large, easy circles, powerful searchlights combing the streets below. Sirens sound and police cars come down the streets, their smaller searchlights darting back and forth, probing the night, which grudgingly gives up a few feet of ground to man's light.

It goes into an alley behind some darkened buildings. A police car turns into the alley. It crouches behind trash barrels until the car is gone. There is a sound near it, a singsong humming. It's from a boy with long hair, lying there, an empty smile on his face, far, far out on some galactic acid trip. It lifts one of the trash barrels and brings it down again and again on the boy's head.

"We've got half the police force out there," Inspector Flanagan protests.

"Get it all," I press him. "It's within a mile radius. It may hide, but it won't run. It won't try to break out of a converging circle."

"Why not?"

"Because it doesn't understand fear. Its needs to attack are too great. Just keep tightening the circle."

For the first time I see that fear is gathering on Flanagan's face. This thing I have built with my words, which he has enlarged with his mind. He might be about to see it.

The police car moves slowly down the alley. Officer Ratchford drives, alone, after receiving the emergency call. He hasn't had time to replace his partner, who is on sick call. As the right front tire goes over a plank with a large nail sticking out of it, the weight of the car drives the nail deep into the tire and the plank into the underbelly of the police car. Officer Ratchford stops the car, gets out, bends over to try to pull the plank loose. A sixth sense tells him to turn, but it is a sixth of a second too late.

Hands circle his throat. Choking, starting to black out, he draws his gun, pushes it into the stomach of the man, and fires three times. Officer Ratchford dies, never knowing why three bullets into a man's stomach don't make him let go.

It gets into the police car and drives out of the alley onto the street, passing other police cars, whose occupants

SIMON'S SOUL

are too busy looking to look at the occupant of another police vehicle.

10:27 P.M. ... Father Ryan sits sipping a glass of sherry. We can hear the noise of the helicopters, the movement of police cars. Instead of providing security, it only makes me aware it is closer.

"It will get here," I say quietly.

"Yes, I think so." Father Ryan sips more sherry, takes a small cross out of his pocket. "Shall I hold the cross up in front of him?"

What the hell am I doing smiling at a time like this?

It drives the police car around the corner and down the street, the street it has been looking for. Another police car arriving is no cause for suspicion. It takes the shotgun from the post and gets out. A man with a shotgun getting out of a police car is not alarming. Things are happening. There has been constant movement and action all evening. It is merely another detective who has arrived in a police car. Hardly a noticeable event.

As it approaches the house, the door is opened by an officer coming out. It raises the shotgun and fires into the officer's head. As he falls, an officer behind him draws his gun and fires at the man with the shotgun. The bullet passes through the man's neck. It fires the shotgun again, and the second officer's stomach is ripped open.

All is bedlam. A half-dozen officers converge on the man with the shotgun, firing.

Stanley Shapiro

We hear the shots. No matter how much you expect it, sudden violence is always more sudden than your expectations. It is here! We sit there, frozen in momentary indecision. Dr. Warner's body comes hurtling through the plate-glass window.

It is on its knees in the shards and splinters of glass. It pushes itself up and stands there looking at me. At the sight of me, it is so overwhelmed by its malignant wrath it opens Dr. Warner's mouth and lets out an appalling, paralyzing cry. In a paroxysm of irate passion, it tries to free the profanity within itself. From out of Dr. Warner's mouth come the head, shoulder, and right arm of evil itself. . . . Its scarred, bloodied face, with the black holes for eyes and mouth, from which molten lava oozes—the arm from which maggots and worms and other diseased insects crawl—the jagged claw dripping blood. It points the claw at me, shrieks in savage execration, and is swallowed back into Dr. Warner's body.

I hear Father Ryan's "Oh, God," and it is upon me, Dr. Warner's dead hands reaching for my throat. I try to pull its hands away. I sicken at the smell of dead flesh, at the corrosive odor that comes from the open mouth. In a blur I see what seems like dozens of hands grabbing at him. It screams and shrieks and howls as hands try to pull it off me.

As double vision meets and becomes single sight again, I see seven or eight men on the battling, twisting thrashing figure. I yell over and over, "Don't hit it. It can't be hurt. Tie it up. Chain it."

SIMON'S SOUL

It battles with a profane energy, but every time it pulls free of one arm, another arm grabs it. One wrist is cuffed and then the other, and they are joined together. . . . And then the legs . . . More cuffs are put on to secure its subjugation . . . and then chains are wrapped around it.

It struggles, fights, heaves bone and flesh against steel. . . . Roars and vicious cries of vile defiance. . . . But it is caught . . . contained.

TEN

11:40 P.M. ... I ride with Inspector Flanagan and Father Ryan to police headquarters. We are following the armored car that it is locked in. Neither Father Ryan nor I speak, for what we have seen is beyond discussion.

Inspector Flanagan quietly says, "What do we do with him?"

I don't answer because I don't know.

A wing of the jail is emptied. Bound in chains, it is put into an isolation cell. The tiny television camera in the ceiling of the cell watches with an unemotional eye.

We sit in an adjoining room, watching it on the small screen as it writhes and pulls and jerks and heaves against the chains, hurling the bound body against the walls of the cell. It is infinite, outraged energy.

The awed commissioner asks the same question Inspector Flanagan had asked, but this time to the right person. "Jesus, what do we do with him?"

They stare hypnotically at this whirlwind of wrath, in

the silence of an emerging fear. They did not really understand at first what they had caught. Now, as they look at it, knowing they will never understand what it is, they start to feel the seeds of terror budding in their nervous systems.

They are looking at something not human. It can't be booked, arraigned, charged, tried, sentenced, and put away out of sight.

It can't be declared insane, for it has far outdistanced insanity as man knows it.

It can't be killed.

It can't be buried. Wait. Perhaps. In a cement coffin, not lowered into the ground but isolated on some remote island, with generations of guards to watch over it, so that if it ever breaks out it can be rechained and returned to another coffin.

And when do we bury it? After arraigning it? After the trial? What public defender will be assigned to defend it? Under our laws it is entitled to counsel. But that applies only to living persons. Will the Supreme Court have to rule on a dead person's right to counsel? I can see some civil-rights groups picketing in protest that we are denying it its inhuman rights.

At the moment, the news media and public are content that I am an insane, murderous physician. I am sure that any number of my former patients are examining their healed wounds for flaws to see if there are any malpractice suits they can throw at me. A surgeon who has murdered four of his colleagues is vulnerable.

Neither do the other myriad murders that have oc-

Stanley Shapiro

curred shock the people. It's the way the world is today, they shrug. Mass homicide by one of its own kind is far more acceptable than a single killing by an alien life.

I can only imagine the hysteria, the chaos, if we were to confirm what we have captured.

The army of lawmen, churchmen, doctormen, and philosophermen surrounding the dead body. It would be the end of the world to many, whereas others would start to react with the ferocity that marked the beginning of the world.

To announce it and show it to the world is unthinkable. We have about forty-eight hours before we have to resort to that due process of civilization that may proceed to plunge us into uncivilized reactions.

In those forty-eight hours we must destroy it. But it can't be destroyed. Then send it back. Back to where? And how? What if it should escape Dr. Warner's body? It could terrorize and tyrannize the earth. Could it bring more like itself to us, through the rent, the rip, we have made in some supernatural tapestry? Could this one rip unravel the entire tapestry?

I am enormously tired. I must sleep, sleep so I can awake to think. I am given an injection.

September 4 . . .

3:00 P.M. . . . I have slept more than twelve hours. What a blessing sleep is. Sleep, our earthly womb, our secret hiding place. A life phenomenon we may never find after death.

Breakfast is brought in. I am so aware, so appreciative, of our earthly life. A hot, vitalizing liquid called coffee, the good taste of toast, the thirst-quenching, hunger-satisfying feel of cereal and milk. A crisp slice of bacon in your fingers. Cups and saucers, chairs and tables, windows and curtains, electric lights and telephones, a bathroom and a newspaper, cognac and cigars, clothes and shoes, plumbing and garbage disposals, running water and moving cars, beds and bathtubs, shaving cream and razors, towels and cologne, mirrors and hair dryers, music and movies and televised words, medicines and markets, teachers and fire-fighters, policemen and priests. And only here on earth do they exist. Everything made by man to make man more comfortable. The comforts of life, which we so rarely appreciate. Heaven and Hell may not even have a toothpick.

Man has slept while nonman has struggled and strained and cursed and hated its way through the night. I have bought new strength with the hours. It doesn't have to replenish that which is inexhaustible. Time is only *my* enemy.

Father Ryan removes a small flask from his hip pocket, fills the small cap from it. "A wee drink in the morning to help me face the world. A stiff drink at night to help me forget it."

He drains the capful in one graceful motion. His face becomes serene as nerve centers are made aware of this welcome guest. "A bit of brandy," he says. "It is the neighborhood friend of the lonely priest. A few capfuls and I can stand to hear a hundred blasphemous confessions. I can survive the assault of a hundred tales of lust and greed, lies and misdeeds."

Stanley Shapiro

I like this little priest. I know that if I am around him long enough, I could be tempted to convert to Catholicism. Not because it would please God but because it would please Father Ryan. It is not the tree that attracts us but the fruit hanging from it.

He listens, he understands, I can relate to him. How fortunate I have a Father Ryan to turn to. It is that thought that gives me the idea. "I wonder if it has its Father Ryan to turn to?"

The old man looks at me, puzzled. I try to explain what is not yet very clear to me. "Not to excommunicate but to communicate. Not to exorcise but to apprise." The flesh of the plan is filling out the bones of the thought. "If it had been a saint who had come to earth, Father, whom would I have taken him to? The church ... a bishop, a cardinal, someone who is a living part of it."

Father Ryan pours a bit more of the flask's contents into where it will do more good. "You're saying you want to try to talk to it?"

"Not me so much as have *it* talk to someone who would understand."

Father Ryan starts to refill the cap.

"Father, do you believe God hears you when you talk?"

He rubs his chin with his fingers as he gives it the deepest thought, looks at me with the bluest, most honest eyes I have ever seen. "Yes, Doctor, I believe He hears me. That doesn't mean He answers me."

"Do you believe in angels and saints?"

He smiles. "I'm Irish. Even the most atheistic Irishman believes in them, Doctor. Aye, I believe in them. Last

SIMON'S SOUL

night I saw a demon come out of a man's mouth. How could I not believe in angels too?"

"And men have talked to angels, haven't they?"

"It's what has made them saints."

"Then if men can talk to God and angels, can't others talk to Satan and his kind?"

He studies the flask. "This looks like a drinking day."

"Are there those who can talk to Satan, Father?"

He takes a deep breath and says, "The Lord himself was forced to. A man cannot believe in Heaven and not in Hell. Or in the Lord and not Lucifer. You cannot quote one paragraph in the Bible and ignore the other." He takes a small pocket Bible out of his jacket pocket. "I'm preaching the Lord's side of this story. There are those who preach the other side." He starts to pace as he talks, partly to me, partly to himself. "It's true. If you were troubled, who would you call for? A man of God. It's trapped in that body. It's troubled. Who would it be calling for? A man of Satan, one of his ministers. You may have a point there, Doctor."

The man continues to amaze me. This simple, ancient Irish priest, whose horizons, at first glance, would seem limited to the miracles of St. Patrick cleansing Ireland of the snakes—his vision blurred by a few too many drinks—his knowledge of the world confined to what he has heard in the confessional—his Irish judgment telling him things are either green or black.

He is an enormous human being, with a tremendous sense of right and wrong, a capacity to accept cosmic theories and yet not ignore the plight of the dandelion. He has the courage to face the enemy of his Lord. Father Ryan, you are a mighty man.

He telephones the bishop's secretary. "A harpy," he calls her, "born to please no man, and making up her guilt by serving a man who is not allowed to please any woman." As he waits, he adds, "She's enough to make celibacy a celebration," then into the phone he says, "Miss McCallister, Father Ryan. And how are you today, my Catholic beauty? ... Yes, I've heard they've caught the one who's been doing all those killings. Sure and it turned out to be your father.... Now, be good-humored, my gray-haired lovely. If your dear father were a murderer, he'd have started much earlier. I've got an important question for you. Remember when Father Thomas did a study on Satanism in Southern California? There was one group considered an authority. We put it on our prayer list, remember? It was headed by a colored woman.... Yes, that was it, the house of Belial. And what was the colored woman's name? ... Isis, yes ... Would you be giving me the address? I'd like to pay her a visit.... Go ahead, Miss McCallister, tell the bishop, but remember, I have powerful friends at the Vatican."

ELEVEN

4:15 P.M. ... The House of Belial is a small converted one-story warehouse in south-central Los Angeles. Surrounded by squalid, rotting, abandoned buildings, it champions this desperate street. Fittingly, all the buildings are condemned, but no one has bothered to follow through on tearing them down, primarily because no one wants to invest in building something else up.

The only force that has kept vandals from ransacking the street, from looting the remains, is the House of Belial. It is something you didn't mess with. You heard stories of what went on inside, and it was enough to make you walk or drive other streets.

The dark gray wooden door is opened by an incredibly beautiful child of about ten. He is deep black in color, with flawless features, as if a master sculptor had painstakingly carved him for centuries and turned the perfect stone to perfect flesh.

Curly hair peculiar to his race, but of gentle texture,

peculiar to other races. Deep chocolate eyes set in seas of white, which blend into the black shores of his skin. A straight Grecian nose, with a slight flair to the nostrils that makes them sensual companions to the lips beneath them, which are soft but firm, partly open, provocative in either male or female. Flawless teeth, too perfect to have grown voluntarily, but set there one by perfect one by that ageless artisan. He wears a black T-shirt and pants. One can sense that the body beneath is equally flawless.

After the last days, the thought of coming here had conjured up visions of ugliness and defilement. It meant more of the horror I had seen. I was not prepared for beauty. I had seen the true face of Satan. Was this child's face but a mask that was being used to lure us into complacency?

He looks at Father Ryan and me in silence. I feel as though I have been examined, appraised, and a conclusion has been made. This child knows more than what he is not saying.

"This is Dr. Reynolds. I am Father Ryan." The boy child nods his head. His continued silence makes his beauty ominous. He turns and leads us down a hallway shrouded in heavy, dark curtains.... Dark curtains like those Dr. Warner had once been lost in ... If there are objects about, I do not see them. Up to a door on which hangs an inverted blood-red metal cross. An inverted cross—Lucifer fallen? The boy knocks once on the door, opens it, motions us in.

It is a large room, filled by the presence of Isis. She sits in the center of the room on a stone chair. On either side of her a tall standing black candle burns. On the walls are

SIMON'S SOUL

objects that have no meaning to me, expect for the skull of what may once have been a dog.

Isis, too, like the boy, does not blend with her beliefs. Delicately frail, with fine white hair ever so carefully parted in the center and pulled back into a bun. Her skin is neither too light nor too dark; her features are neither too white nor too black. Enough wrinkles to show great age but not enough to show weariness. She wears a simple black dress, the kind I remember seeing a French singer, Edith Piaf, wear. A thin mesh chain around her neck from which hangs a small carved ebony spider. A ring on each index finger. It is her eyes that dominate the first impression. They are peaceful eyes.

"I am Isis." The words come softly but with a strong sense of identity.

"I am Father Ryan." The little man opens the skirmish with an introduction. "And this is Dr. Reynolds."

She sits quietly, waiting. We have not approached her out of friendship. She will not start the conversation out of friendship.

"We have come for your help, Isis." Father Ryan opens the chess game by losing a pawn.

"Why should I help you, Father?" Lightly spoken, but the first indication of a deep hostility.

"Because we have captured one of your kind."

"And we many of yours."

It is the dialogue of two minor ambassadors, each speaking on behalf of his all-powerful majesty. Each confident his lordship would triumph in the ultimate battle.

"We want to send him back to his world."

"You have your rituals, Father."

"He is beyond them."

Father Ryan takes a pawn with that. There is a slight stiffening of her body as her interest has become our captive too. Her slender finger stroke the spider, and I see it is not carved at all. It is moving its legs. How strange that, as terrifying as my last days have been, a live spider on a woman's neck is almost as shocking. The spider has wrapped its six legs around a finger, as a child its arms around a mother.

"Talk to your God, Father."

"I would rather you talk to yours."

A smile as she takes another piece from the chessboard. "You are afraid of your prisoner."

Father Ryan moves a piece to neutralize the advantage. "His loss will be a greater blow to you."

Her eyes, those kindly, gentle twins, turn to me. "You haven't spoken, Doctor."

"As the architect of this tragedy, I would rather let others do the rebuilding." She nods her head in understanding. I cannot help but add, "I cannot equate what I have seen to your relationship to it."

She smiles. "I do not appear to be my religion's keeper?"

I am honest with my answer. "I cannot believe that you pray to such horrors, that you represent it, that you would wish it to triumph, that you would wish yourself to become like it."

"Well said, Doctor." Father Ryan is pleased.

"But not well thought out, Doctor," the old woman

SIMON'S SOUL

counters. "Yes, I am the believer, the practitioner, the guardian of everything you call evil. It is part of the balance. Life and death, love and hate, pious and profane, creation and destruction, they must be balanced. They are all held together by opposites. Neither God nor Satan can exist without the other. It is necessary for there to be opposites, else there would be no balance, and without balance, nothing."

Perhaps she is speaking monumental truths in simple comparisons, but that would make them no less truth. I will reply in simple truth. "We have captured evil. We do not know how to communicate with it."

She crushes the spider between her fingers. White blood runs from it, down onto her dark skin. "Bring him to me."

2:00 A.M. . . . The armored car that it has been put into, followed by the police cars, turns onto the street of the House of Belial. Deserted by day, it is an area of desolation by night. One functioning street lamp casts a light that does not seem to have the strength to reach down to the ground, causing a black mist to float above the sidewalk. If there is an earthly shadow of the valley of death, this is it, and as we drive through it, I am afraid, for I know not who are the shepherds here, what kind of troubled waters we will lie down by, or whose house we shall dwell in.

The door is opened by the beautiful black boy. He is wearing a black suit, black shirt and tie. It must be his Sunday best, or the best he wears for whatever day he honors.

Stanley Shapiro

The steel door of the armored truck is opened. Evil emanations, malicious auras, gush out. The sickening odor of decayed death, rotting flesh, seeps into the wet night air. It is brought out, thrashing violently, jerking the body held by chains.

As they bring it to the door, the child falls to one knee and bows his head.

Straining, heaving against its bindings, cursing unrecognizable curses, it is carried into the House of Belial.

The moment it passes over the threshold, it ceases struggling. It is an abrupt shock, this sudden passivity. This violent, virulent, outraged force suddenly serene. Of course. Wouldn't an angel from heaven feel secure if carried into a church? This is his embassy. He is now on the property of his homeland.

The child leads us down the darkened corridor but not to the same door. He pulls a hidden cord, and curtains part, revealing a larger door made of some metal. It casts a glow, not of the richness and purity of gold or silver but of some raw, base, malignant matter. It is not an earthly metal. It has come from some foundry that deals in incredible foulness.

We enter the prayer room, the holy chambers of this opposite religion, this spiritual balance. A thin, cutting wind blows in a circular motion. There are rows of wooden pews, although when I touch one, it does not have the feel of wood cut from a living tree. It has the hard, cancerous feel of something atrophied for centuries beyond count.

A narrow semicircle, with a cold, concretelike floor,

SIMON'S SOUL

leads to an altar. An eight-sided wall is behind the altar, with eight candles on it, each emitting a heavy green flame. On the walls are hung or painted what look like circles and squares and triangles, with forms that are not identifiable as human or animal but, rather, a combination of both. On the altar is a stone slab, about four feet high, three feet wide, and seven feet long. Next to it is a smaller stone slab on which lies a small dog, not of any breed I can identify. He is held by a thin leather strap on each paw, and over his mouth a muzzle, tightly fitted so that he cannot howl. All that comes out of him is an almost inaudible whine of fear.

To the side of the altar is something that I can identify only as an old church organ, yet different in that the sides of it taper to points, and there seem to be far too many keys on the keyboard.

The voice of Isis comes softly, from nowhere and everywhere. "Lay him on the offering table." He is placed there. Dr. Warner's chained body lies there, quiet, unmoving. That violent storm of energy within him, where has it gone? Is it gone?

"All except Dr. Reynolds and Father Ryan will leave."

Inspector Flanagan starts to protest. Father Ryan holds his hand up. It is truly a father's hand, raised in a silent authority that demands total obedience. Inspector Flanagan and the officers leave. The door swings closed behind them. The holy chamber is sealed off.

"You will sit in the seat of the lower witnesses."

The only seats are the pews. Father Ryan and I step down from the altar and sit in the first row. It is harder

Stanley Shapiro

than wood, harsher than metal. One cannot feel any evenness. It is like sitting on a blanket of nailheads.

The child seats himself at the organlike instrument and begins to play. A sound comes out unlike any I have ever heard. How can a musical sound be profane, savage, maliciously unclean? It grates against the ear like a piece of iron dragged across a sidewalk. It has no harmony, no rhythm, no melody, but somewhere, somewhere beneath this teeth-grinding sound there is a song, a song written before there was music. I can think only of the old woman's statement about balance and opposites. For music there must be antimusic, therefore this antimelody is pleasing to certain ears. I am grateful no one is singing the words to it.

Isis appears, wearing a scarlet robe. Across the shoulder and down across the breast, a snake has been painted. I remember the spider and try to focus on the snake through the green glare. It is indeed moving, across her breast and up across her other shoulder and back again around her neck.

She approaches the dog, takes a small, razor-sharp sword from an unseen compartment of the slab it lies on. In rhythm to the sound that is coming out of the organ, she begins to chant in words I cannot understand, but words that almost bring Father Ryan and me up out of our seats. There is an unknown meaning in them, so deeply antihuman that the sound of them is like an attack on mankind itself.

I cannot absorb it. I cannot bear its hostile meanings. I am about to yell, to scream, to cry out to her to stop,

SIMON'S SOUL

when she raises the sword and strikes the dog's head from its body.

The shock of her action freezes me to my seat. She takes the head, dripping with warm blood, and places it on Dr. Warner's chest. I hear Father Ryan's intake of breath, but I cannot turn to him.

The ungodly music, the mind-assaulting words, the dog's head on the body—it is ghastly, and yet it starts to assume a mysticism, a presence, a religion, a god. I am beginning to sway back and forth as though I am a helpless appendage of this unknown power.

She opens her hand, and a coarse purple powder falls from it onto the dog's head. A thin fog starts to emanate from the mouth of the dead animal and spread itself over Dr. Warner's body. She takes the snake from her shoulder and sets it down on the slab. It slithers into Dr. Warner's mouth and disappears.

She cries out in her unknown language in what must be supplication. The green glow of the candles intensifies till we are sitting in a brilliant green glare. There is silence, and then the deep bass, grinding voice I have heard, again comes from Dr. Warner's lips. Not in shrieks or howls but in a harsh, rasping staccato flow, in that same senseless, sinister language the old woman has spoken.

At the sound of the voice, she loses her mastery. She falls to the ground and grovels in panicked prostration. She writhes on the floor, in reptilian humiliation, the lowest of the low, the least of the least, the most undeserving of the undeserving. She tries to claw her way into the earth, to bury herself, to hide her ugly presence from the sight of the supreme being. The child's fingers feverishly pick out keys and chords never created by man. Unclean melody blends with obscene words. Their song is whole.

The voice stops, the green candles dim, the child strikes three final chords and sits silent. The old woman rises, removes the dog's head from Dr. Warner's body, places it next to the body it was cut from. The snake emerges from Dr. Warner's mouth. She lifts the snake and places it on the dog so that its body coils like a collar where head and body have been separated. She passes her hand over it, and when she removes the snake, the dog is whole again, lying there as before, uttering inaudible whines.

She walks to the edge of the altar so that she is but a few feet from us. She is the high priestess again or witch or sorceress, but apparently shaken by the revelation.

As she stares at me, I almost detect a trace of awe in her voice. "You have captured the son of Belial."

TWELVE

"The son of Belial?"

Father Ryan, bless his stout sanity, interprets for me. "Belial is Satan himself. One of his names, like Mephisto, Asmodeus, Lucifer, the fallen angel."

"Never fallen, Father," Isis says quietly, "and never an angel. Belial and your God were created at the same time."

Balance. Opposites. My reaction is one of incredulity. "How could we have captured the son of Satan?"

"In the same way you captured and killed the son of your own God," she answers. "Once your Christ was in human form, he was bound to its human limitations. Dr. Warner's soul belonged to Belial. When it did not arrive, Belial sent his son to learn why. Something like this had never happened before."

"Where is Dr. Warner's soul now?" asks Father Ryan. "I would like to pray for it."

"Send your prayers to Hell." She turns again to me.

Stanley Shapiro

"He entered the body, not knowing the mind was still alive. The agreement between Belial and your God is that each may work on man's mind, but neither may enter. Once inside, he became part of it and could not escape."

No wonder it had howled and raved, become a maddened wind of destruction. The son of Satan trapped in a human body, unable to contact his own kind until we brought him to one of his lower followers. His rage was the rage of wanting to be free. Those murders, those macabre multilations, were ordinary, simple, natural acts. The balance. Opposites. Absolute morality, absolute immorality. Divine love, divine hate. He was simply exercising his side of the balance.

"He must be freed to return to his father." She states an irreversible fact. "Anything less is unacceptable to Belial."

God gave his only begotten son to save the world. What would Belial do to get *his* son back?

"Aye, that's why we're here," says Father Ryan, "to give him back."

"He has destroyed thirteen," she says. "He has delivered thirteen souls to his father. The agreement is to receive souls, not to deliver them. It must all be balanced. Thirteen souls must be delivered to your God."

She stares at me. Her eyes have become part of her religion. Pillars of marble. My reflection is distorted, not in sweeping curves but in sharp angles. To look beyond her eyes would be like walking through barbed wire.

Father Ryan was not staring into her eyes but into her

words. "And how will thirteen souls be delivered to my Lord?"

"Through Dr. Reynolds. The architect of his entrapment must be the instrument of his release."

The balance.

"The boy will point out the thirteen."

"God almighty." The words rush out of Father Ryan's mouth like a soft wind into a surging forest fire.

"Belial almighty." The old woman balances the scales.

I will have to kill thirteen people. The child has walked up to Dr. Warner's body and is touching his forehead to Dr. Warner's forehead.

"He is being given the knowledge to select."

"No!" The words were Father Ryan's. "There will be no more killings."

"A joyous occasion for those killed, Father." She smiles. "They will be going to your Heaven."

"Let them go when they are due."

"They are due now."

"No." It is goodness answering evil. "To murder is to sin. That is *your* God's name. The man shall not commit murder."

"Even to send thirteen souls to your Heaven? For that is where they will surely go."

"Even to do that, for he shall be doomed to Hell."

"No, Father, your God will raise Dr. Reynolds to the side of his angels." Before Father Ryan can protest, she continues. "For you, Doctor, will have saved your God's life. If Belial's son turns to nothingness, so shall Belial, for they are created of the same force. If Belial vanishes, your God vanishes too, for they were created to exist together or not at all. If they cease to be, everything in the universe ceases to be. Everything that was, is, and will be shall be nothing."

"Something has to remain." I am desperately trying to reason out a something that existed before the beginning. "The power that created Good and Evil."

"It divided itself into each of them. Nothing will remain." She turns to the boy, who stands behind her. "Show him your hands."

The child steps down to me and holds his arms out, palms upturned. One flawless palm, cut from the purest gold, without a single line to mar its perfection. The other palm holds ten thousand lines, deep, jagged, twisted lines from which a stench arises.

"The child is the symbol of the balance, of the agreement between the two gods, their acknowledgment of each other, of their differences and their oneness."

The child returns to her. Lifting the sword with which she had decapitated the dog, she slashes at the child's wrist. Before we can cry out, the hand with the golden palm drops from his body. The child begins to moan. Crackling, sizzling energies and counterenergies twist his body. The skin on his face develops gaping fissures as atoms start to loosen their grip on one another. The hair falls from his head, and his skull begins to split slowly into two sections. Small bolts of fiery energy leap out of the cleaved skull as the universe of his body explodes,

SIMON'S SOUL

disintegrating into nothingness. Only the two hands, palms upward, remain on the altar floor.

"Without the balance, he has ceased to be."

The hands desperately drag themselves across the floor toward each other until the fingers of each touch. They clasp each other and the boy stands before us, whole again.

"Millions of souls in eternal torment will cease to be, Father, but so will millions of souls in eternal peace. God and Satan. Heaven and Hell. They exist together or not at all."

There is fevered urgency and command in her voice, as though an unseen hand were inside her body manipulating her like a puppet, using her to speak its words. "It must be now ... Now ... They are aware of the imbalance."

"Who is?"

"Our gods. They cannot hold it together much longer." Her voice is quite low, with almost an echo effect. "They are afraid, Doctor. They do not want to become nothingness. They do not want to die. They have no souls, only themselves. They want to continue. Blessed shall be the soul of the man who saves them." Her words are aimed at my consciousness. "Your God wants you to save Him, Doctor. Save Him and He will save you."

Soulless gods, godless gods, all will continue or vanish into a never-ending forever. Was God crying out to me, asking why His son has deserted him?

Her voice penetrates my thoughts, casting them aside as

a tidal wave a floating branch. "The child will point out thirteen. Slay them."

"Father Ryan! Dr. Reynolds!" Inspector Flanagan's voice is riding into the storm my mind is tossing on.

He comes into the chamber, followed by another detective. The sight of us, of Dr. Warner's body, soothes the panic he has just experienced. "The door . . . the door you came through . . . It wasn't there. I swear to God, it wasn't there, and then it was there again." His orderly mind, which deals in terms of yes and no, good and bad, the law and the lawless, can never truly comprehend powers beyond legally constituted powers. It is the type of protective simplicity that has saved police officers their sanity. When confronted with what can be mind shattering, they do not reel under the trauma, they merely say, "That is illegal."

"Are you all right?" he asks. I nod my head, and then I am sickened to the very core of whatever I am, appalled to the pit level of my awareness. The child is pointing at Inspector Flanagan.

THIRTEEN

6:10 P.M. ... Father Ryan stares at the pointing child. The old woman cries out, "Now, Doctor! It must be now or it is all over!" Inspector Flanagan has a puzzled look on his face as I reach up, take the sword from her, turn, and plunge it into his body. In a shrill voice I cry out, "One."

The other detective is immobilized. He looks at the dead inspector; he looks at me as though expecting me to apologize and say it was all a mistake. The child is pointing at the detective. While he is waiting for me to explain, the sword enters him. I hear myself say, "Two."

Father Ryan, by rote, is kneeling beside Inspector Flanagan, giving him the last rites. I want to laugh. "What are you doing?" I cry out to him.

He looks up at me from his robot-like position, from his rehearsed words. "They don't need any last rites," I yell. "They're going to Heaven."

My words become his thoughts, almost as if he is

staring at himself, at his useless, needless invocation. Of course. Why is he interceding for a soul already in Heaven?

There is an air of futility about the old priest and his collar. The look of a man who has just been told the tools of his trade are archaic.

The old woman opens a door between two green candles that I had not seen before. She doesn't have to instruct me. I go through it, a man with a mission. Eleven more souls to deliver to my God. The child, a silent creation of the universe, is behind me. Eleven more souls to deliver to my God. So God and Satan, Heaven and Hell, yesterday and tomorrow, will remain.

The child takes my hand with his God hand and leads me from one sightlessness to another, until I feel the street under my feet, the night in my nostrils. I do not know what street I am on. It cannot be far from the House of Belial. We pass swiftly through alleys, silently across shadowed streets. He suddenly stops and, with Satan's hand, points.

Sitting against the steel-shuttered doorway of a store is a man's figure. Asleep or drunk I do not know, but he is asleep or drunk the last time on earth. I thrust the sword into him, and Heaven has another soul.

"Three," I whisper to myself. God forgive me for the way I have to save Him.

More alleys, and finally through a door and up loosely boarded stairs. Another door and I am in a room. A candle is lit. I wonder why there are always candles in the house of the gods.

SIMON'S SOUL

It is a bedroom, the child's, I must assume. A mirror hangs on a wall. In it I see the reflection of the candle. It is upside down. A wooden cross hangs in front of the mirror. Its reflection is inverted and not of wood but of that base metal. That balance, that intricate, immortal balance.

If there are windows, they are covered by shades. A four-poster bed sits exactly in the middle of the room. The top of each bedpost is a carved head of some animal or demon, fearful to behold.

A bed, a mirror, a candle, one door. My eyes become acclimated to the dark shadows. The child opens the door. It is a closet. Hanging in it is the skeleton of a child.

It is dressed in the clothes the child wore when I first saw him.

It is his skeleton. From what century, what life? Or was it before there were centuries and life? Just as we keep old toys when we have long outgrown them, sentimental trophies and memories, he keeps this skeleton.

I almost lose sight of him as he walks into a corner of the room. He returns carrying a glass filled with a liquid, which he offers to me. I drink it without smelling or tasting. I have long passed the point of caution. I swallow it and start to laugh. "It's Seven-Up . . . Seven-Up."

Still laughing, I sit down on the bed and start to undress. Seven-Up . . . Seven-Up . . . three down and ten to go.

September 6 . . .

I am awakened by movement, by an engine's sound. The ceiling is a few feet above me, the walls about four

Stanley Shapiro

feet apart, and I am lying on a mattess on a floor. I am not in Heaven, for Heaven couldn't be this cramped. And I am not in Hell, for this place is merely uncomfortable.

I am in some kind of camper or trailer. Sometime during the night I was moved. I feel the metal side of the vehicle. Its rear window has been curtained, as is the space between the rear section I am in and the driver's section. I get to my knees, reach over, and part the curtain. The child is sitting next to the driver, a man in his early thirties, who is either a white man with an Afro hairdo or a black man with white skin.

It is dusk outside. Could I have slept that long? Was something slipped into that simple Seven-Up? We are slowly cruising down a Los Angeles street. At least I must presume it is Los Angeles.

And every person walking that street must be aware of my existence. Dr. Reynolds, a physician of past repute, whose mind has snapped, who has killed well over a half-dozen people. Is there an order to shoot me on sight? Will my son volunteer to be one of the hunters?

The old woman will be questioned but not too closely. We are too religious a country to put much stock in Satan's actually existing. We believe too deeply in the Hereafter to have the Hereafter confirmed. We adore God, but it frightens us to come face to face with Him. We are Christians afraid to prove our Christianity. It's why we don't look at funeral processions too closely when they go by, and why we'll meet people outside of restaurants and stores but not outside a cemetery. We glance the other way when we pass a mortuary and are relieved when an ambulance disappears down the street. We are spiritual people who do not examine the spiritual, mortal people who do not believe mortality will ever end.

Father Ryan? Can he actually tell anyone what he has witnessed? Can he tell the bishops and cardinals that he saw the devil's son, that it is in Dr. Warner's dead body, that it killed all those other people, and that God will cease to exist if I do not deliver thirteen souls to Him? Poor Father Ryan, to know so many secrets and keep them secret still.

Dr. Warner? They will perform an autopsy. Officers will swear he was alive when they carried him in and dead when they carried him out. Another murder chalked up to Dr. Reynolds, who also slew Inspector Flanagan and a detective while making his escape.

They will puzzle over the bloodless body, the bullet holes, the ripped flesh and broken bones. The old woman will not talk. Father Ryan cannot talk. A dead puzzle cannot be kept lying around too long. They will bury it and the secret within it. To try to understand would be madness. They will be content that the madness is mine.

We drive till dark and finally stop. The rear door is opened by the child, and he leads me into the rear entrance of St. Bartholomew's Church. It is Father Ryan's church.

Down the basement stairs and into a small storage room. Amid the clutter of worn church fixtures is a carved wooden figure of Christ on the cross. The child makes the sign of the cross with his God hand and a strange rectangular sign with his Satan hand.

Stanley Shapiro

The Christ figure is quite old, the toes broken off, one elbow chipped, the nose cracked, and the paint faded from its body. I've never thought of it before. What do you do with a worn-out Jesus? You can't throw him into some garbage can. You have to hide him.

Who makes them? What man goes into the business of mass-producing Christ on an assembly line? Does he go home to his family after work and say, "I made four hundred and twenty-five Christs today," or "It was a good week; we sold three hundred Jesuses"? Is the man mad at God's son if he doesn't sell too well? is there a good month and a bad month to sell Christ? Is Christ built to break, planned obsolescence?

The child sits on a stack of old Bibles that have been piled up in a corner of the storage room. The door opens and Father Ryan comes in. We embrace, a long, wordless embrace. When two people have shared a monumental experience, there is no need to verify it to each other. Their embrace is their total recollection.

"I've prayed for you, Doctor."

"I think God is praying for me too, Father." Gallows humor? Irreverent? Perhaps, but desperate men use desperate phrases in order to smile.

"Are you hungry?"

God, make sure you bless your little Irish priest too. In the storm's eye, where men must hang on to their Gods, their beliefs, their sanity, their lives, where eternity is a fact, where creation itself may be destroyed, he still worries whether I am hungry. I have heard jokes about the Jewish mother. He is my Jewish priest.

SIMON'S SOUL

He brings me sandwiches and milk. How good, how very good it is. Yes, the balance. The supernatural and a sandwich. Eating evens up eternity. How good life is. Why hadn't I taken the time to enjoy it more?

I finish eating, and Father Ryan produces another mortal gift, a fresh cigar. I light it, sit back against a broken pew. I am at peace. If I could but spend the remainder of my life here, with ham sandwiches, good cigars, and Father Ryan's company.

We are soldiers in a foxhole, and at any moment the order will come to rise up and kill again. It is now when soldiers tell each other secrets they have kept from family and friends. A time for idle chatter and intimate confession.

"I was born in Shannon, by the sea," he says. "An Irish Catholic, which automatically made me a member of the first people in the first country of the first God. That I would be a priest was settled early. I was not strong enough to let my body earn its way, or wise enough to be one of the chosen of the lower class to attend a university, or handsome enough so that the women would make my celibacy a constant test. My strength has always been an inner self that was content to live life in the body and mind God gave me. I was born to die a priest. My books were God's books, my toys were His words, my joy His life, my life His death, my future His past.

"Aye, there's a smugness in knowing you know. I was a walled stronghold, able to defend against any attack. But every fortress has a weak stone that rattles against the firm ones. It was this stone that witnessed babes born with crippling diseases, lame bodies, and useless minds. Children caught in airless closets, under moving cars, down in swimming pools, and up in bedroom fires. Young people dying in error and in war, by man's anger and nature's fury. Old people perishing in pain and fear, poverty and loneliness, so frightened, so alone they have forgotten they were once the proud possession of their parents. If God is love, how could He allow such suffering? And that stone in the fortress trembled and shook. But now we know, Doctor. The stone has been cemented to its brother stones. God is not all-powerful but half powerful, not fully responsible but half responsible. There is now an explanation for the horrible things I could not understand my God allowing. He hasn't. I do not have to explain His mysterious ways. Those mysteries are not His doings. That He rules only half a kingdom makes that kingdom more desirable. That God Himself is vulnerable makes it more urgent that He continue to live. Don't you see, Doctor, an absolute God must be held absolutely responsible. There were irrational things no rational God could allow. His lack of absolute supremacy makes him absolutely supreme. Half a God who is perfect is better than a whole God who is flawed."

I look at him, this priest, whose fortress faith has been battered by incredible facts and who stands stronger than ever in half a kingdom.

I look at the child, of dubious human creation, an emissary from both Heaven and Hell, who will help me erect thirteen murderous pillars to support Heaven and Hell in a proper balance, and when they are balanced, he may simply burst into two halves of nothingness.

SIMON'S SOUL

I look at myself, the only man who can save God. More than a knight going forward on a holy crusade to serve his God and save his soul, I am going forward to save my God and serve my soul. ... The child touches my shoulder. The time has come.

I give the cigar to Father Ryan to hold for me. A symbolic gesture, like the light we leave burning at home, a place to return to.

9:40 P.M. ... The child and I have walked through alleys for perhaps forty or fifty minutes. Why haven't I seen a police car? Are they all so busy looking for me they have abandoned their normal routes, the alleys and back streets that are a criminal's highways? Are they driving along the main boulevards and broad avenues of the lawful masses, hoping the instincts of my upper-middle-class life will make me travel familiar roads? Are they at my home, at airlines, bus stations, hotels? Are they wasting critical numbers in noncritical places?

The rears of small neighborhood stores stand firm on each side of the alley. Yea, though I pass through the alley of the shadow of death, I shall not fear, for both the Lord and Satan are with me.

The child stops at a barred store window. He points. It is the back of a printer's shop. The child opens the rear door and we enter.

I have left the sword in the church. The child did not remind me of it. It was meant for only three lives.

The printing machine guns out invitation cards like square white bullets. Will this machine also print the sympathy cards the printer's widow will send? I pick up the heavy wrench with which he has often fixed a faulty

Stanley Shapiro

machine. Don't look around. I mean you no harm. Tonight you shall be in Heaven. I am saving it for you, your father before you, his father before him, your son after you, and his son after him.

I bring the wrench down with enormous force on his head, sending splintered bones into a brain that is never aware it can no longer think. The blood tumbles out of his mouth and nose, forming grotesque patterns on the birth announcements. "Four."

We enter a three-story medical building, go up the fire stairway. The child opens the door and points. The man is a night cleaner, mopping a still-wet floor. A black man in his early thirties, well over six feet in height and two hundred pounds in weight. How do I kill him? With what do I kill him? I have left the wrench in the printer's shop. Why don't I carry a permanent weapon? Am I depending on some divine and undivine guidance to provide me with the death tool for each particular soul?

This man will not die easily. What if he should kill me? If I die, God dies. Why has the child selected a victim who can destroy us all?

I advance toward this large, muscular man, unarmed. He continues to clean the floor, his huge hands controlling the mop as effortlessly and as gracefully as a conductor his baton. There is an art, a rhythm, a silent symphony of cloth and water and tile.

The fire hose is wound in a tight circle on the wall, like a giant coiled snake with a wicked metal head. Next to it is the fire ax. Remove it . . . be careful . . . be quiet . . . be quick . . . He will turn any second now. . . . A few more

SIMON'S SOUL

feet ... raise the ax ... if he doesn't hear you, surely he must sense you. ... He turns as the ax comes down. The hearing aid falls from his now totally useless ear. Now I know why he didn't hear me. The balance. This superb body destroyed by an ear that couldn't serve it. In Heaven his hearing will be perfect. "Five."

The woman has bought a morning paper from the coin-operated news rack. She walks into the small corner coffee shop, emerges carrying two small cartons of coffee and wrapped pastries.

The parking lot has a dozen or so cars in it. Hers is a '67 Pontiac with worn tires.

She opens the two-tone blue door, puts the coffee container and pastry on the plastic seat cover, gets in, closes the door, and opens her purse to search for her car keys. I lie quietly on the floor by the rear seat. The motor turns over in fatigue. Before she can shift into gear, I raise myself, throw one arm around her neck, and grab her hair with my other hand to pull her head back. She tries to suck air into closed tubes. Her bulging eyes look into mine, and she tries to make them say what her lips cannot. Why? Don't ... Stop ... I want to live. ... She knows she is dying, and she doesn't want to. I try to console her. I speak softly, soothingly. "It's all right. It's really all right. Your soul is going to Heaven. Please believe me, you'll be with God in just a few seconds." Her eyes are begging me now. I try to ease this final moment. "It's all right. Trust me. Trust me.

"Six."

I pull the body over into the backseat, climb over into

the front seat behind the wheel. The child comes out from behind a parked car and gets in next to me. We drive off.

11:45 P.M. ... We have been driving for half an hour down streets picked at random, at times main arteries, where our headlights are cones in a beehive of headlights, at times on deserted roads, where we are solitary stalkers, our muffler sounding the low, ominous roar of the night hunter.

The child points. The young man is riding a Honda motorcycle. As I pick up speed, he doesn't turn, expecting me to go around him. I go over him.

The car bucks and bounces as we press cycle and cyclist into the ground. I make an illegal U-turn in the street. Strange that I should remember I could get a traffic ticket for that. I slowly drive the car over the still-twitching body.

"Seven."

12:15 A.M. ... We drive down Sawtelle Avenue, alongside the Veterans Cemetery. For the first time the boy does not stare straight ahead but turns and looks at the endless rows of crosses. Is he counting souls, which went to God and which to Belial? Do they balance out?

The engine's cough joins the muffler's cough. The gas-gauge arrow rests on EMPTY. Old cars don't die, they just run out of gas. Why do I think of a terrible pun like that? Why do I think of General MacArthur? Of course, the Veterans Cemetery. Is the general in Heaven or in Hell? The child knows. I don't ask him. If I ever talk to him, I want the first question to be of monumental importance.

The residue of gas and fumes at the bottom of the gas

SIMON'S SOUL

tank is sucked up into the gasping engine. It manages to push us into the Chevron station. We stop behind a middle-aged man in a Lincoln, waiting for service. He raises his car window to ward off the noises that come from the radio of a Mustang that is parked by another pump.

Three boys and two girls are in the Mustang, keeping time to the music as it raucously attacks the night with Elton John's voice. They are of college age, all dressed in jeans and assorted sweaters. The driver has an unlit cigarette in one hand, and his other hand is tapping on the dashboard. One boy, his arm around one of the girls, whispers in her ear, and they both laugh. They have many years of laughter in front of them. They have their entire lives in front of them, until the child points at them.

I get out of the Pontiac, walk up to their car, pull the hose out of the gas tank of their car. The gas is gushing from it. I put it into the window of their car and start to spray them with it. . . . They scream as the gasoline floods their eyes, as the poisonous liquid runs into their mouths and noses. They claw at blinded eyes; their screams become choking, vomiting sounds as their lungs become burning ovens. It soaks their hair and their clothes and the cloth of the car. I take the matchbook out of my pocket, strike a match, and toss it into the car. Five human, raging fires are started. As their charred bodies thrash, the burning flesh of one attaches itself to that of another, like rubbery, blackened marshmallows.

The hysterical middle-aged man has jumped out of the

Lincoln and is running down the street screaming. I get in the Lincoln; the child follows. As the attendant runs out of the rest room, we are already leaving. In the rearview mirror I see the fire increasing in size, the black smoke of charred bones and car-seat stuffing mixing with the orange-red of purer flames.

"Eight, nine, ten, eleven, twelve." I am amazed how simple it is for someone to kill a lot of people.

FOURTEEN

1:45 A.M. ... I abandon the Lincoln on Olympic Boulevard and take to the back alleys again. From the sky the floodlights of police helicopters pinpoint pieces of ground. The staccato wails of sirens echo against one another.

One more and God will be saved. Why is the child leading me back to the church? Is there time to finish tomorrow, or is the final soul in the church? Please, please, don't let it be Father Ryan.

We enter the church, and the child leads me back down into the basement storage room. As he resumes his seat on the stack of Bibles, I lie down in an abandoned pew, and in minutes I am sleeping.

September 7 . . .

8:00 A.M. ... The light has somehow managed to squeeze in through a split in the boards that cover the basement window. The morning beam touches the scarred, deteriorated figure of Christ on the cross. Old gods never die, they just end up in the basement. I've got

Stanley Shapiro

to stop with variations on a saying that was a verbal assault on lofty quotations when it was originally spoken.

The aroma of hot coffee turns my head. Father Ryan is sitting on an old crate, holding a tray on which is my breakfast. His eyes are discreetly riveted to the floor. He knows now as well as I what occurred last night.

I take the tray from his hands. They are trembling. I return to my pew and eat my breakfast. The child sits on the Bibles, in the same position I last saw him. Without food or drink or sleep. He does not micturate or defecate. From the time I first saw him I have not spoken a word to him or he to me. Has he a voice, or is he a mute double agent of Heaven and Hell?

Father Ryan has the beads of his faith between his fingers.

"One more," I say quietly.

He nods his head and speaks in equally restrained softness. "They came last night while you were gone, to see if I was safe."

The thought sends sudden sharp bolts of fear through my body. I glance at the child. Don't point at Father Ryan.

As if he is reading my thoughts, Father Ryan says, "It will finish here in the church." He too senses why the child brought me back. "If I am chosen, Doctor—"

I do not let him finish the thought. "No! Not you, Father! I would let God die first!"

"And in so doing, hurt me the most. I have spent my life preparing to meet Him, to come before His glory, to kneel before His love, to spend forever in the sweet shadow of His presence. I have lived to die for Him. Would you deny me the purpose of my life, Doctor?"

We both turn to stare at the sound of a blade cutting chips of wood. From some unseen pocket the child has produced a small silver pocketknife. He has picked up an old wooden cross, perhaps two feet in length. He is whittling an end of it into a point. The last victim will have the cross driven into him.

The child works carefully, methodically, until the point of the cross is needle sharp. He walks to me and hands me this holy weapon. Father Ryan is praying silently to himself. The child opens the basement door. We follow him down the basement corridor, up the stairs into the church. A death procession going to the execution, but Father Ryan's step is quick, sure, almost exultant.

On to the altar. The child faces us, lifts his arm, turns, and points off.

He is pointing toward the empty church seats. No, not totally empty. In a pew, on her knees, a small girl, perhaps ten years of age, is praying. The same age as the child. Opposites. Balance. The Devil's hand is toward her.

Father Ryan gasps. "No, not the girl. She is in a church. *Me.* Take me." In desperation he grabs the child's arm. "Let *me* die."

The child looks at Father Ryan, and his mouth forms the most obscene smile I have seen. His teeth are tones of violent purple. Small, fierce white blotches mar his black skin. He shakes his head no.

"But I want to be with God," the old man pleads. The child shakes his head no again, and Father Ryan's face

Stanley Shapiro

pales with the implication. He is suddenly very vulnerable. It is hard for him to form a sentence he never imagined. The words comes out in spurts of spiritual pain. "Doesn't my God want me?"

The smiling child shakes his head no.

As Heaven vanishes, Father Ryan's entire body begins to tremble violently. He pronounces the sentence on himself. "I . . . am going . . . to Hell."

The child nods his head yes.

Father Ryan, bones melted, sinks to his knees and then to his hands. He lives, but the life has gone out of him. His breathing is gasps of agonized despair. The words, caught on the tail of the despair, are pulled out of him. "Oh, God . . . Oh, God . . . I am going to Hell."

I want to scream to the Heavens and beyond, to wherever it is they are. No! Not Father Ryan! Not this gentle, holy man. Not this trusting Irish soul. Not this most Catholic of Catholics. Not this old man who gave his youth and his years to his God. You can't balance him out of Heaven.

He is on all fours, like a whipped dog, sobbing into deaf ears, "I love you, God, I love you."

What sort of God am I saving? I kneel by the old man and rest my hand gently on the white hairs. "I will not save Him, Father. If He would send you to Hell, I shall send Him to oblivion."

But the heart that gave itself to its Lord will not falter now. "I have sinned. I have offended Him."

"When, Father, when? How? Where?"

In bewildered honesty he sobs, "I don't know, I don't

SIMON'S SOUL

know." In steadfast loyalty he says, "He is God. He is fair."

The child touches my shoulder with his God hand. I push it away in anger. "No more. I shall kill no more. If God can survive without this man, then let Him try to survive without me."

From the rear of the church I hear the voice of Isis. "Finish your work."

She stands at the top of the aisle, the left side of her dress black, the right side white. She walks down the aisle toward the small girl, who has been sitting there in fear and fascination at what she has seen and heard. Isis says, "Finish your work and I shall explain."

"Tell me first," I shout at her.

"First the girl," she replies. "The girl and then the answer."

The answer. The search for the answer that started so long ago. She is right. I cannot stop one soul short of the answer. I step down from the altar and up to the girl, who sits there staring at me with those wide, wide little-girl's eyes. She stares at the pointed cross and watches as I drive it into her chest.

In great bitterness I say, "Thirteen."

I hear that horrifying shriek once more. The son of Belial is in the pulpit. Blood on his head, boils on his body, exuding pus, worms and maggots crawling in the holes, molten fire oozing out his eyes ... Father Ryan's future master.

It shrieks again, and the body of Christ falls off the cross and shatters.... The black child begins to shrivel and spiral into himself until he loses all human shape. It writhes on the ground, snakelike, and the snake breaks into thirteen pieces, and each piece becomes smoking flesh and then becomes nothing but wisps of smoke. The abomination raises its clawed arm toward the sky, utters some horrendous, triumphant profanity, and is gone.

Father Ryan lies on the altar floor, withered, wasted.

"It is balanced," says Isis.

"The answer. The answer," I shout at her. "Why is he going to hell?"

Isis steps up to the altar, looks down at the weeping priest. "Because he is Belial's messenger."

The old man shakes his head and cries out in anguish, "No, I serve my God."

"And Belial is your god," she replies. She looks at the walls around her. "The church is Belial's. *His* creation, his domain, his house. Churches and temples, mosques and pagodas. All religions belong to Belial—to bless warriors and war, evil-doers and evil, sin and sinners.

"The Bible," Father Ryan moans. "The words are God's words."

"They are Belial's words. It was he who wrote it. He mixed gentleness with terror, love with hate, promises with threats, all to confuse you. He wrote, 'Thou shalt not kill,' and then told you, 'An eye for an eye.' He wrote of peace but talked of battles. He praised wise men, but fools were his kings. He showed each group a different path to salvation, and each path led to him. The Bible is Belial's sword, cutting off man from his fellowman."

She looks down on the crushed priest. "You so easily

forgave trespasses, which only led the offender to trespass again. You blessed those going forth to join the slaughter. You sustained yourself with the coined offerings of murderers and thieves. You erected your churches on the dollars and desires of greedy, rapacious, arrogant donors."

I am trying not to lose my parents' beliefs. "The church belongs to Christ."

"Only the name on it. Christ had no church."

"He built it on Peter."

"On men, Doctor. His church was man, not walls. Each man's salvation lies in himself. Each man is religion itself." She condemns Father Ryan. "You prayed to God, but you served his enemy."

Father Ryan, rocking back and forth on hands and knees, is still hostage to his life's rituals. "Forgive me. Forgive me, God."

"He will not."

I cannot bear the agony of the man, the destruction of his living spirit. I walk up to the fallen Christ figure, whose pieces lie scattered on the altar floor. "He loves you, God," I shout at the pieces. "Why didn't you tell him, warn him? You allowed him to be misled."

There is no answer from God's fragments. I turn to Isis. "Is not the Bible itself warning?" she asks. "Are not the words and deeds so vile that you did not stop to wonder?"

"We were raised to believe," I protest.

"And did you honor your God when you believed He brought upon the earth terror, consumption, blindness, and sorrow? Did you worship Him when you believed He caused wild beasts to devour children? When He urged men to break the bones of their enemies and eat their flesh? Were you worthy of your God when you believed He did truly say, 'I come burning with anger—lips full of indignation—sword filled with fury and blood, to destroy, to make of the earth a furnace of affliction. ... I am jealous, vengeful, wrathful, fierce and hateful.' Did you truly want to follow a God who said, 'I created evil'?"

She is right. She is right. Oh, that book, that book that made a demon out of our Deity, and we believed. We dared to call fury fairness, hate holiness, lechery love, and murder judgment. How could we believe in a God with a split personality—who kisses and kills, caresses and curses? God or the Bible. One is true, one is false.

"Man wants to be misled," she says. "Every instinct tells him to be wary of the praying masses, of masses chanting hymns. Every instinct tells him the church is a constructed contradiction. Every instinct tells him that the confessional is not a conduit to God but an alley to self-deceit. Every instinct tells him that God is closer than his nearest church. But man has not the courage to trust himself to judge himself, for he knows the sins he has committed and the sins he will commit. If man were the final judge, he could not allow himself his errors, so he lets others judge. He delivers his soul into the hands of strangers. He comes to Belial of his own free will. Do not blame your God for deceiving you. You have deceived yourself."

Father Ryan pushes himself to his feet. He is speaking to his own ears. "Forgive me, God. If I have not served you, it was because I did not know. I go to Hell still loving you."

He has opened a Bible and is tearing out the pages. "If the Bible offends thee, I shall cast it out." He begins to twist the torn pages into a torch. "If the church is thy enemy, I shall destroy it."

He has struck a match to the pages and holds the burning words aloft. "Praise God. Damn his enemies." He puts the flames to the tapered red curtains behind the pulpit. They start to burn.

The church is burning. Stained-glass windows crack into stains and glass. Father Ryan climbs into the pulpit, which is now ablaze. As the flames start to engulf him, he looks up toward his lost Heaven. "Good-bye, God. I love you."

Isis is sitting in a pew that is beginning to smolder. Flames and death are her friends.

I walk out of the fires of the church and sit on the lawn. I see the approaching fire trucks and police cars.

FIFTEEN

December 25 . . .

I have told my story many times, to the police and lawyers, psychiatrists and bishops. I am not even brought to trial but instead taken to this barred room, where I am told I will spend the rest of my life.

The room is bare except for a bed, washstand, and toilet. I am watched while I eat and while I write these notes. A minister comes once a day to pray but leaves when I keep trying to tell him he is doing Belial's work.

No one understands.

They will.

I cherish the hours I have to myself. It gives me time to work on my plan. It is very complicated, but when I meet God, as I shall, I think there is a way to get Father Ryan to Heaven without disturbing the balance.

PART II

SIXTEEN

April 14 . . .

4:25 P.M. . . . Tomorrow I shall commit suicide and meet God.

Is God a man or a woman or both? Has Jesus been balanced out? For a Christ born to the Virgin Mary, was there also a Christina born to some virgin father who, never having consummated the act with his lady, could not understand how she gave birth? And did this Christina child grow up, the daughter of God, filled with supernatural senses, having to speak eternal truths in the kitchen, working unseen miracles while cleaning the bedroom, explaining redemption to the livestock in the barn? Was inattention, anonymity, and a patronizing smile the cross she lived and died on?

What cross are you now on, Father Ryan? From burning church to fiery Hell. As it scorches your soul and you cry, "Oh, God," does that name act like oil on the flames? How much better if you had become a village fisherman

Stanley Shapiro

and gone down off Shannon by the sea and God had raised your watered soul to the heavens. You deserved Heaven, not the priesthood and its hell. God must be aware that you served only Him. I will tell Him so tomorrow. The morning of my death shall be the evening of your departure from your suffering.

You shall see God, Father Ryan, I promise you. He will catch your tears, and they shall each turn into a diamond, and He shall string them on your lifework for Him and wear it as a necklace as a reminder of your love for Him.

God owes me a favor, and the favor shall be that He and His brother exchange my soul for yours. Yours to be raised to Heaven, mine to be lowered to Hell. The balance retained, and each of us in his proper forever. And which of them will argue this exchange? God shall be rid of a murderer, and Belial shall receive the one who almost destroyed him. Surely he will have a choice punishment for me, who snared his son and endangered his very existence. A Father Ryan is no challenge to his horrors—just another priest among a myriad of holy men, assigned to standard eternal torments. Even infinite evil eventually has to run out of infinite variations. The unbearable punishments, with passing eons, must eventually take the edge off the beast's joy at the horrors he creates. He needs a special soul to rekindle the profane flame that rages within him. A soul that will renew his savage spirit, inspire him to reach deep within his malevolent self to create a hell for me that will make me envy Hell as it now exists.

Death holds no final fear for me, merely a fear of where

SIMON'S SOUL

it shall take me. It is not an eternal void but a sentry station at a border, where we are directed to new destinations. I will see Heaven and then Hell, the first soul to be so honored and then humbled. From one's rewards to the other's revenge. Is the torment there more than one can bear? Can the soul survive Hell?

Will I see Dr. Simon Warner and Dr. Mannis and Dr. Carlson and Dr. Blakely? Will we have a chance to congratulate ourselves on our findings?

In my brief moment in Heaven, will I see all those I murdered? The woman, the students, the black man, the child? Will my apologies now be accepted? Will they thank me for where I have sent them?

Earth seems such a distant place, a city I have passed through in my car and yet still see in my rearview mirror. The mirror is my life. Tomorrow I shall break the mirror.

My earthly body is a burden that I drag along as I hurry to the future. It is an antique that has served its purpose, of only sentimental value now. A modest apartment I have lived in, but I am moving to new mansions.

"You have visitors, Doctor." It is the guard speaking from behind the bars—the bars behind which he is imprisoned on this earth.

It is my wife and son.

My son has a flash camera in his hands, and as I turn to face him, he snaps the photo, and the bulb becomes a minuscule atom bomb, its blinding glare destroying all feelings I have for him. In his world a photo of the insane doctor is worth a minor fortune. I have become more than a father. I have become a financial asset. He has struck gold in our blood relationship and he shall mine me for every dollar he can salvage. One day he shall write a book about me. He shall be given a fat advance to remember our thin relationship. Out of respect he will probably call it *My Father, the Murderer*. His dad, the human slot machine, will no longer pay out in nickels and dimes. I will have become the jackpot.

No longer merely the capitalist surgeon who sold out to the law-and-order establishment—I have become the idol of every freaked-out, fucked-up nonconformist. As they plunge the tainted needle into withered vein, flooding their blood with that deadly mass, they are going on a Dr. Reynolds trip. In the cluttered chaos of gray coffeehouses, my name rolls off corrupt tongues, onto torn tablecloths, and up to the low ceilings, where it is lost in the thick pot smoke. Guitarists, playing with drugged abandon, write songs about me with social intent and nasally sing them as juvenile junkies keep time by beating some invisible rhythm in their hidden minds. Wealthy anticapitalists open their landscaped villas to law-hating lawyers, who raise funds to free me and all other oppressed murderers. I am their new hero. Why I killed is of no importance. That I killed is what makes me worthy of the affection of this self-mutilating minority. The less obvious the motive, the more glorious the deed. The zenith of the nihilist. I am the anti–folk hero. A burden to my wife, a boon to my son. As I languish in a cell, he luxuriates as a budding celebrity. With his twelve-inch cock and his two-inch morality, his will be done, in the bedroom and the bank.

He is taking photos of me from every angle. On his toes,

shooting down. On his knees, shooting up. Flashbulbs waste their instant lives, like silver-cellulose soldiers, in one burst of brilliance, dying to promote the ill-thought-out scheme of an ill-thinking king.

Acting the madman he is now the proud son of, I reach through the space between the bars and try to knock the camera from his hands. "You son of a bitch," I scream, "I'm not an animal. Don't feed me. Don't take my picture." I point to the open toilet bowl in the corner of the cell. "You want to take a shot of me sitting on the can? How much will you get for me taking a crap?"

"Ben!" My wife recoils in distaste. A stupid smile spreads across my son's face, like an incoming dead wave across a deserted beach. A shot of the mad doctor on the john. It would be worth thousands.

"Get him out! Get that son of a bitch out!" I am screaming. "I hate him! I hate the bastard!"

"Ben, please." My wife's words want to calm down a minor family fracas in the dining room. She does not seem to understand it is the last room I shall ever dwell in.

"Ungrateful, stupid shit! Get him out!" As my son is led away by the guard, he stares at me, a thick smile exposing his large, arrogant teeth. His revenge on me will one day be in the chapters of his book.

I grasp the bars with both perspiring hands and lean my head against one of them. "Why did we have him?" I ask my wife. "How did we have him? One of us has recidivist genes. We re-created the cave man."

"It's not easy for him, Ben." My wife's loyalties are

subtly shifting from father to son, from past to practical.

"When has it ever been easier for him?" I reply, biting into the acid taste of truth. "I'm a killer, insane, imprisoned forever. These are the best years of his life."

She has not responded to the words "killer" or "insane" or "imprisoned forever." She has made no token denial, if only for my benefit. For almost eighteen years she has been the perfect wife—the mate even the most devout chauvinist could not fault. Home and husband have been the haven of her heart. I have been her harbor in life's storm. The pier she tied her life's ship to.

Then, one day, with the peace of mind only a faithful, fruitful, dutiful wife can possess for a job well done, she would go to her God, to serve Him with the same devotion in Heaven she had given her husband on earth. Oh, the beatific serenity of a good woman who has fulfilled God's expectations of her. Was the Virgin Mary afraid to go and face her God for judgment?

My wife's life and death had been perfectly planned—but only under perfect life-and-death conditions—for her perfection is a smooth, closed circle that cannot contain within itself the sharp, angular cutting edges of murder and madness. Like a sickness within the body that the body must cast out, I have polluted her circle and must be expunged. The phlegm of my deeds must be cast from her throat, which sings only God's song.

The sanity and survival of all good, simple people lie in the ability of instant withdrawal, in abruptly changing course without remorse, in erasing yesterday and not allowing the past to go back any further than today.

Her ship of life is turning its engines over. It is slipping

SIMON'S SOUL

loose the hawsers that have held it to the pier for eighteen years. It will back into the mainstream once again. At forty-two it is not too old to find a new berth. And, being a good woman, a decent woman, she will serve this new man with the same loyalty that once was mine, providing the man orbits within her God circle.

She cannot help being what she is, a good woman. I will not press on her circle, asking to reenter, but I cannot deny myself that momentary luxury.

"Are you afraid of me, darling?"

"Why would I be afraid of you, Ben?" she replies, staring fearfully toward the floor.

"I explained why I had to kill them, didn't I?"

"Please, Ben—"

"You believe in God, don't you?"

"You know I do."

"Then why can't you believe I did it for Him?"

Now that she can speak for God and not for herself, it gives her the courage to face me. "God would never ask you to kill for Him, Ben."

"He didn't want to die."

Stealing acting techniques she has seen on television—oh, how secure our everydayness makes us—she puts her hands to her ears to shut out the blasphemy. "Stop it! Stop it! God can't die, Ben!"

"Why not? If He can be born, He can die."

"I'm going to leave, Ben. I'm not going to listen to you." She welcomes this proper excuse to cut loose the last lines holding her to me. "You're sick, Ben. You're a very sick man."

"You're my wife and I love you."

"I don't want to argue, Ben."

"Argue about what? That I love you or that you're my wife?"

"You're twisting my words," she says as she tries gracefully to twist free from me.

"Do you love me?" I ask.

This will be the final line she has to cast loose. Face-to-face rejection of me. "I'm all mixed up, Ben"—and the final line floats on the water.

"Yes or no. Do you love me?"

"I don't know." The winches are drawing the line onto the deck of her life ship.

"I want to make love to you."

"Ben, please."

"Lots of prisons permit it. It can be arranged. Here in the cell, for an hour."

"In the cell?" She recoils in horror.

"You and I. Oh, we've had some wonderful times together. Remember? You'd wrap your legs around me—"

"Ben—"

"And we'd turn over and you'd sit on me."

"You're disgusting."

Disgusting. Her ship is backing away from the berth. What was once divine is now disgusting. I want to sink her, sink her before she sails away. "All right, not in the cell. Just back up against the bars, darling, and lift your dress. Remember how you used to beg me to do it that way?"

"May God have mercy on you, Ben." Each word a saw

SIMON'S SOUL

tooth, cutting even memory between us. And she is free, she is gone. Go in peace, wife. Let her find happiness one more time, for she is capable of giving happiness. Yes, I would have liked making love to her one more time, and once again, before I die.

SEVENTEEN

April 15 . . .

Sunday. The day we pray and pay to the God we have created—half Christian, half currency. Sunday, the day even the shut-ins are not shut out. Even the thankless can give thanks. The unremembered are permitted to remember. The lost are given permission to find themselves. The poor can feel pity for those beneath them. The infirm thankful they are not the insane. The insane above those in the ground. And those in the ground pray for those trapped above it.

What is there to be thankful for in this cell? Its steel and concrete walls barely able to hold the man, much less his joy. Containment cannot hold laughter. The bars are not wide enough to let a smile through.

Abolish all prisons! Served time does not save time. For the minor crimes, minor tasks like collecting garbage, cleaning rest rooms, servicing sewers. Let the offender's sentence be to clean up after the offended. For the

SIMON'S SOUL

heinous crimes, no cells, but exile. Total exile—to an island that they can never leave—with no one to watch over them but themselves. Let them be their own law. Let them commit every offense they wish against one another. Their island, their laws, the terror of their thoughts. Let it be a place of such horror that before one commits a crime of magnitude, he will pause and weigh the crime against the conviction—to be sent forever to this island where there will be no society to protect him from his peers.

12:45 A.M. ... There is one thing I must do before I die. One last earthly defiance of Hell. One belligerent gesture—a twist of the tail—a tweak of the nose. Mortal irreverence. Let Belial froth at the mouth at the thought of getting his claws on my soul. Let Father Ryan's soul be a small price to pay in exchange for getting mine.

"Guard," I call out to the man sitting on the wooden stool at the end of the corridor, half asleep.

And the guard calls back, "Yeah, man, what is it?"

"Today is Sunday. I want to pray to Christ."

"Ain't he got enough problems?" Then the Christian elbows aside the cynic. "Go ahead and pray, man."

"I have nothing to pray to." Thou shalt not worship graven images. I rely on man's nature, that reality is more real if you can see or touch it. On man's inherent fears and doubts of things made up only of thought. How can I pray to a God I can't see or touch? *That* a man can understand.

"Get me Christ," I cry out. "Somewhere, in some office, on some wall, lying on some desk, you can find him."

"Okay, okay. Don't lose your cool," he mutters as he

goes off to search for Christ. He does it for selfish reasons. God won't forget this deed. The guard is piling up day-of-judgment points.

He does not hesitate in leaving me momentarily unwatched. I am secure behind the bars, and he is secure in knowing I have been a passive, patient prisoner, never having spoken too loudly too often. I am a man who has gotten all his murders, all his hate, out of his system and is now content to write his memoirs.

He returns carrying the figure of a wooden Christ on a wooden cross. It is about a foot high and seven or eight inches across.

"Here you are, man." He hands me God's son.

"Where'd you find him?"

"In the captain's office, laying in the drawer."

"Thank you. The Lord will not forget you for this." The guard nods his head, reassured that his internal motives will reap eternal rewards. He goes back to his stool at the end of the corridor, sits down to contemplate the meaning of Sunday to a black man. A white God, white mother, white son, white angels in white gowns. Has Martin Luther King, Jr., become a white saint? I cannot tell him that Martin, in all innocence, was a courier of Hell's news, that he preached Belial's book. The blacks, those great churchgoers, they've been had again. Not free at last in Heaven but slaves again in Hell. Is there equality of opportunity in Hell? Is everyone allowed to suffer equally, regardless of race, creed, or color? Does Hell have the tallest basketball team?

I remove my cotton prison pants and shirt, and silently begin to tear them into long, narrow strips. I knot the

SIMON'S SOUL

strips together. I have accepted death and suicide, but the hangman's rope still leaves me squeamish. There is something about putting your head through a noose and then stepping into air, to thrash and jerk and then dangle, lifeless, that erodes all dignity. . . . Like a side of beef hanging in a slaughterhouse. Like a featherless chicken in a butcher's window. At least I'll have my shorts on. Hanging naked is an insult to all life forms.

I hold Christ on the cross in my hands. How Belial has mocked us all these centuries. God's son. Not free, not triumphant, not a figure of authority but a pinioned prisoner, nails driven through him, head bowed in despair, God conquered. Instead of human outrage at this symbol of God's defeat, we suffer servile acceptance of Belial's arrogance. Oh, Belial, you clever, cunning power. You even have us praying to the bare cross itself. We carry it, like a tiny, deadly anchor, around our necks, and it drags us down, down, down to you.

Are we so blind that we cannot see that the cross is not a godly symbol but an ungodly sword? Turn it upside down and it is a weapon one can hold in one's hand—a blade Belial uses to fence with God as they battle for our souls, as he parries, lunges, and thrusts our souls on it like meat on a skewer.

The cross, a symbol of savagery, and we have been tricked into kissing it. It stands sentinel above every church. The ministers make its outline on their chests. There is really no sleight of hand here, no masked misdirection. Belial has openly, brazenly told us the church is his, and all within it belong to him.

But let Hell's master know there is one who has seen

through him. My Christ will not remain prisoner to that dreaded cross. I will free him.

8:25 A.M. ... With my fingers I have worked on the wooden nails that pierce the wooden flesh, that hold him to the wooden cross. I have loosened them sufficiently so that I can slide the edges of my fingernails in the openings, and I pry and pick and pull at them. My nails break off where they meet tender flesh. I am in pain and I have lost my tools. I use my teeth. As I try to free Christ, I am kissing him, honoring him.

The punishing nails are shaken loose. I once again use my fingers' strength to finish the emancipation.

The nails are out! I lift the body of Christ off the cross and gently lay it down on my pillow. I stand the cross against the floor and wall, and with the heel of my shoe I break it. It is destroyed with a loud snap—a snap heard in Hell—and Belial winces and awaits me.

Christ is free! How peaceful he lies there. How powerful, how wise. How can you follow a captive? How can you believe in a man at another man's mercy? How can you pray to defeat? The cross, the crescent, the Hebrew star. They are Hell's bell, book, and candle. They toll for, read for, and burn for the Unanointed One.

Christ lies on the pillow. Who was he really? Was he the virgin son of a virgin mother? What were his true thoughts, his true fate? I can no longer trust the Bible, with its half-truths and whole lies, its tarnished heroes and glittering villains, its failures and fruitions, its carnal lust and spiritual solemnity, its sword and its sanctuary,

SIMON'S SOUL

its old wives' tales and young men's dreams, all mixed together, shaken well, and poured—into Hell.

I take the hangman's rope and attach it to the small overhead fixture. I will soon know the answers. I test the knotted cotton for strength, stand on the toilet, put the rope around my neck, and step off the bowl into forever.

1:40 A.M. ... The noose pulls blindingly tight, reinforced-cotton hands grip my throat. The pain is sharp, piercing, extremely unpleasant. Worse than the pain is the sudden abrupt closing of the air door between mouth and lungs. The last breath released, no more to be drawn. I try not to cry out, but strange, inhuman, nasal grunts force their way out. Lungs frantically try to recycle the already rotting air within, in which is now a poisonous, burning vapor. It sends its toxic contents into my panicked bloodstream.

Air—life's ultimate ally. My chest is being crushed. My head is one enormous, splitting headache. My tongue reaches out beyond my lips, desperately trying to scoop chunks of air into my throat. My eyes are fogged with spheres and jagged lines. Where is death? God, but it's hard to die slowly.

Oh, Simon Warner, whose soul we searched for. We have opened sacred doors and been inhaled by a giant breath—whirled madly about in cosmic lungs—and been spit out—human dots on an infinite chessboard. We lie there helplessly as pieces as large as solar systems are moved about at dizzying speeds. I do not understand the game or why it is being played—but it is a game, and

Stanley Shapiro

though I am an invisible speck on that board, somehow I can influence the outcome.

But first I must die. Life is not a plus in posterity. Dead men may tell no tales, but they create the tales that live men speak of.

I cannot breathe, I cannot swallow, my throat's door is forever shut. I cannot vomit. My stomach's gall is forced back down into its convulsing sac. The thought flashes through my mind that one must never eat a heavy meal before hanging. It is extremely uncomfortable. Oh, God, oh, God, how can one still think of creature discomforts even at the moment the creature is dying?

I cannot see. Am I now where Dr. Simon Warner was, with the black curtain surrounding me? The pain has broken through physical boundaries and is now audible. My head swells and is bursting with a howling, shattering intensity. I cannot think, it is too painful. Let it be Heaven, let it be Hell—either is better than this. Let not my punishment be eternal dying.

I hear the voice in the maelstrom, a clear pond in the savage storm. "Why do you want to die, Doctor?"

It called me doctor. Do our professions die with us? Is Kennedy called Mr. President? When a TV repairman dies and goes to Heaven—no, to Hell; all TV repairmen will go to Hell—does a voice say, "Here comes the TV repairman?"

I cannot speak. I aim my thoughts toward the clear pond. "Is that you, God?"

"I am not God."

SIMON'S SOUL

"Then why are you speaking to me? It is God I am dying to meet. It is God I wish to speak to."

"You cannot speak to God from Hell."

"Am I in Hell then?"

"Close. Quite close, Doctor."

"But I am going to Heaven. Who the devil are you?" If I could bite my tongue at that faux pas, I would.

"It is not your time to die yet."

I am filled with immense anger. I have suffered too much not to die. It is my life. Who is this voice to tell me I cannot take it?

"You saved God's existence, Doctor. He wishes you well."

"Then let him wish me dead. I have business with Him."

"You have business only in Hell."

"Not true." I shout my irate thoughts at the clear pond. "I was told I would go to Heaven."

"Who told you?"

"The woman Isis."

"A follower of Belial. What made you think she spoke the truth? Since when is truth Hell's raiment?"

A sudden fury comes over me, directed at myself, the sort one feels at a racetrack when a horse you had given much thought to but did not bet on comes in and pays a big price. You are angry at not having followed your instincts. Of course the thought that Isis was lying had entered my mind. Why had I dismissed it? Only one answer can make the deaths of those thirteen tolerable.

"If I had not killed," I ask, "if the balance had not been corrected, would all have vanished?"

"True."

What a magnificent, consoling, healing word "true" is.

"Then what was the lie told me?"

"About your soul and Heaven. The woman was fearful that knowing you would go to Hell would tempt you to destroy it first."

I feel betrayed and also a sense of injustice, of ingratitude. "I saved God's life, and He will let me go to Hell?"

"He has no choice," the voice assures me, but I do not feel assured.

"But I saved God, why can't He save me?"

"It is part of the agreement."

"What agreement?" I scream my thoughts back toward the calm waters. "Those Commandments. Who has lived who has not broken them? Who is left for Heaven?"

"The rules are fair, Doctor, fair indeed."

"What about Father Ryan?" I throw this good man's soul at the voice rather than mine. "A gentle, loving man who was tricked by Hell."

"Then be angry with Hell, not God."

"How was he to know the Bible was not God's words?"

"I am truly sorry," the clear pond replies.

My thoughts are withering acrimonies. "Sorry is not an excuse for a God. Without me there would be no Heaven for Him to hear me from. If I go to Hell, it is for Him. I resent that my sacrifice does not merit the effort of His saving grace."

"There is nothing He can do, Doctor."

SIMON'S SOUL

"Not true, not true." I try to believe. "A God always has an alternative. He gave us ten stone Commandments and told us to climb them to Heaven, but we slip because man cannot grab on to stone, and so we cling to our instincts. They are all we can hold on to. If we hold on, we fall, and if we let go, we fall. Would God have become God if He had been judged by the Commandments? Do you demand more from man on earth than it took to create a God in Heaven?"

"There is the balance, the agreement."

"That is not a good enough answer, sir. A God should be wise enough to make a better agreement. We're only human. The road to Hell is not paved with good intentions but with good intentions carried out. ... Are you listening?"

"I am listening, Doctor."

"What of the man who honors his mother and father by honoring their Bible and their church? What of the man who kills to protect the innocent? The man who steals to feed a starving child or lies to save a life or someone's sanity? And aren't there evil souls in Heaven?" I shout. "Men who have honored their parents but gave no love—who never killed but watched in fascination the war's progress—who never lied but destroyed with the truth—who never stole but took all through the powers of the laws they created—who never coveted, for no one around them was left with anything to covet—who never committed adultery but whose wives and husbands lived in frustration and loneliness?"

The calm pond is silent.

"Where is God's guidance to counter Hell's misguidance? There must be a way for God to warn us. Let Him show himself, for goodness' sake. Righteous power not used is power misused. If we walk false roads, build us the true one."

If I could weep I would do so, but I cannot even remember my face and the eyes in them. And where would the tears come from? I am dying, betrayed, Father Ryan is in Hell, and all because I wanted to prove God's existence.

Why couldn't I have left unwell enough alone? Dr. Warner, Dr. Blakely, Dr. Mannis, Dr. Carlson. Why couldn't we have tended to our scalpels and concerned ourselves with saving lives rather than discovering souls? Why did we act like self-pronounced Christs in white gowns and sterile masks, using our quasi-secret caducean confederacy to invade fields foreign to our authority?

Father Ryan would still be alive today. That magnificent mortal, still believing in his Heaven, still dreaming of his chair in God's banquet hall. This godlike man, wanting not to be a God but merely to serve one. My thoughts are desperate thoughts, irreverent. "God owes me a favor."

"They cannot be granted in Heaven."

"I will not accept that." I hurl my desperation at the unknown. "Let Father Ryan's soul be sent from Hell up to Heaven."

"It has never been done."

"Let the powers think of a way. Let all remember I was their salvation."

SIMON'S SOUL

"It will upset the balance."

"That is their problem, not mine."

"It cannot be done."

"I do not believe you."

The waters of the pond become mirror still. "I do not lie."

"Then let me die. If Heaven is helpless, let me talk to Hell."

The calm pond dries up; the raging storm engulfs the site it stood on. The pain becomes grotesque, and all is darkness.

11:47 A.M. . . . What is a round clock doing on a wall in Hell? And what is the sign beneath it that reads DAYLIGHT SAVING TIME? Is forever made up of hours and minutes? Is Hell on a nine-to-five schedule? Is it a winged, black-robed rat race? Does Hell have interns with white jackets and stethoscopes?

"That was a close one, Doctor," Hell's intern tells me.

The soreness in my throat chokes me, as though I am trying to swallow a thorned piece of meat. My words come out one by painful one. "Damn you . . . Damn you for saving me."

He is a young doctor, in his early thirties, but his hairline has already surrendered half his scalp. He has counterattacked the unseen enemy by growing an enormous mustache that hides his upper lip beneath its orange-red bristles. An intellectual walrus.

He sits himself on the edge of my bed and ever so carefully touches my bruised, swollen, welted throat. "I'm Dr. Roman. We were worried about you."

Stanley Shapiro

"Go fuck yourself," I half bark out. An absolutely incongruous, asinine remark but soothing to the psyche. Go fuck yourself. It says so much so quickly. It leaves no doubt as to how you feel.

As his fingers probe the wound, his words open up new ones. "If the guard hadn't found you . . ." He shrugs, "Maybe another few seconds."

A few seconds. Even forever is determined by seconds. Damn that black guard who had saved me. I wish him Heaven, and I wish it segregated. Damn that black asshole. Do they think they ingratiate themselves with us by saving us or serving us? We're all racists toward colors not our own. I cried when I read *Oliver Twist*. Would I have cried if Oliver Twist were black? I think not.

"My, but those are nasty marks, Doctor," says the other doctor, and he smiles with the orange mustache hiding his upper teeth, so only his lower ones show, giving him a fishlike appearance. Has he even got an upper set of teeth? Does that mustache hide some terrible dental catastrophe? Does he have to eat by scooping at the food with his lower jaw like some orthodontic steam shovel?

I read the small button on his jacket: GAY POWER. Had he lost those upper teeth in some monumental sex disaster? I mustn't let him go for my prostate. A gay doctor in a prison. He has found his niche.

"You fucking fag," I rasp out vindictively, irrationally. I take out my anger at God on this human, who has the power to let me live or die while God Himself is powerless to change my life or alter my death. "You son of a bitch. I'm going to shove it up your ass."

SIMON'S SOUL

"You see," he replies with a quietly seductive smile, "I knew we'd get to be friends." He has a sense of humor about being queer. "I practiced obstetrics for three years," he explains. "I delivered two hundred babies. You look into two hundred vaginas, you'd become queer too."

It's difficult to be angry at a man who returns insults with self-deprecation. Not sarcastic, but saddened, I say, "I wanted to die."

The stethoscope is on my chest, enlarging the beat from within. "What would your dying accomplish, Doctor?" he asks, his fingers holding my wrist, testing for the life pulse.

A fair question, with a painfully unfair answer. My dying would have accomplished nothing, except create another Hell soul. Oh, Isis, you infamous, blasphemous, credible liar. You convinced me of a tremulous God, helpless, friendless, fearful of oblivion, of an end so complete it would wipe out even His beginning. To die is an affront to the ego, but never even to have had the ego ... Oh, Isis, you sophistic, antipious fraud, you had convinced me that even though Heaven's door be closed to me, God, in His gratitude, would sneak me in a side entrance ... and once I was inside, He would willingly pay the price of His life, my soul to be exchanged for Father Ryan's soul.

Isis, you perjuring Pharisee, I was a babe in deathland, and once you closed the portals, I could never return again. What a grinding, galling bitterness invades every cell of mind and body. I held God and Belial in the palm of my hand. One squeeze and they would have popped, like pricked bubbles, into nothingness. And if the mighty ones had said a soul exchange would upset the balance, I should have said, "Exchange or perish. Find a way or forfeit your days." Oh, what maleficent comminations sweep my racked consciousness. I had them and I let them get away. I let them off the hook and baited myself.

Dr. Roman's plump fingers are probing into my lower stomach, pressing human organs that play the sounds of life. "Believe me, my friend," he suggests as experienced and expectant fingers examine my lower groin area. I think what this man would give to have my son as his patient. My Cro-Magnon son with his supermagnum penis. I can imagine the headlines: PRISON DOCTOR FOUND WITH RECTUM RENDERED ASUNDER, JAWS DISLOCATED, BUT SMILING.

"Just believe me," he reiterates, his amber mustache masking the mouth. "There are worse places to spend a lifetime in than a prison."

"Easy for you to say," I cruelly reply. Harsh but true. A prison, a homosexual haven. Surrounded by a captive audience, he can pick and choose his lovers, knowing they'll still be there the next day. And if he should want a lasting affair, he simply has to select a gentleman serving ten to twenty.

Either because of medical decorum or personal disappointment, he withdraws his searching fingers. He knows what I have been thinking, but he is not offended. "I've had my lovers, Doctor. What is the difference in choosing someone behind bars or someone sitting at a bar?" He stands and adjusts the needle feeding liquid energy into

SIMON'S SOUL

my body. "There are indeed worse places to spend a lifetime. In a crippled body or a twisted mind." A twisted mind. He throws an embarrassed glance at this slip of a practiced tongue. I've caught his embarrassment and want to milk it for what it is worth.

"Do you think I have a twisted mind, Doctor?"

Whatever emotional tightrope he walks, he is not off balance for long. "I'm not that familiar with the details, outside of knowing you murdered sixteen or seventeen people. Not that I hold that against you. Hell, Hitler and Stalin and Mao murdered seventy or eighty million, and we considered them heads of state."

An interesting thought. I just haven't killed enough people to become respectable. Old Harry Truman—he dropped an atom bomb and he is considered a man with grass-roots instincts. Dickie Nixon varoomed a lot of Vietnamese but he still has plenty of folks who think he was sandbagged. On that logic I can still hope to be President one day, on the ticket the country's been waiting for. The War Party. Elect me and I'll bomb the shit out of everyone. I'll call myself an aggressive conservative. In my gut I know I've got ten or twenty million votes to start with.

"I killed for a good reason," I answer defensively.

"Most people do," he replies in shadowed meaning.

I do not know whether he is understanding or underestimating me. He rolls with the punches, he absorbs words and deeds like a giant sponge. You hurl anger at him and it disappears inside the walrus face, without retaliation. All that wrath going in and nothing coming out. How does he get rid of it? Does he blow it out his ass at night in one huge, indignant fart? Damn him, let him absorb this one. "If I hadn't killed them, the entire world would have disappeared."

The son of a bitch is unflustered. He seems sincere when he asks, "How would it have disappeared?"

There must be some way to rattle the bastard. "You see, God and Satan—he's called Belial, that's his real name—they have an agreement."

"Yes?"

"Which soul goes to Heaven and which to Hell . . . And if the rules are broken . . . they call it the balance . . . if they are broken by either side, then everything vanishes, including God and Belial."

"What sort of agreement?" There isn't a trace of cunning or disbelief in his eyes. Jesus, are the only two people who believe me an old Irish priest and a fag doctor? One is in Hell and the other works in Hell's anteroom. Little by little, I start to tell him the whole bloody story.

EIGHTEEN

2:15 P.M. ... He has listened to it all without smiling, sneering, doubting, or debating. Using absolute silence as a lure, this human sponge has sucked the entire story out of me. I cannot tell whether he has digested it in his hidden inner self or disgorged it. He just sits there and stares at me hypnotically, his large brown eyes like two caged honey bears behind thick horn-rimmed glasses.

"I'm a nut, huh?"

In reply, he opens his jacket, then unbuttons his shirt. On his chest is tattooed Christ on a cross. "I put it on because my brother said Christ hates fairies. He shared a bedroom with me and would rip down the cross I had over my bed. I had this put on and told him to try to take it off."

For the first time I see emotion. A tongue comes out from behind the mustache and nervously licks the edges of the orange-hued hairs and, I presume, the lip behind it.

"The son of a bitch used to run down the street waving girls' panties and tell everyone I wore them."

"Did you?" Damn, I can be cruel.

"Of course I wore them. I was never a closet queen, Doctor. The point is, would you run down the street waving your sister's panties? He'd find pictures of nude men I had hidden, and he'd send them to the priest. It really didn't matter. I'd been confessing to him for three years. He finally decided the problem was bigger than ten Hail Marys, so he recommended to my folks that I go to a psychiatrist. For the next year and a half the psychiatrist and I were lovers. My parents were paying forty dollars an hour while we lay on the couch together, and he'd kick back twenty dollars to me. I saved up enough to pay my first two years' tuition at college. That hypocritical shit brother of mine calling me a fag and playing with himself in the bathroom. I told him I'd rather beat someone else's meat than my own. I don't think my parents really cared one way or another. They were very progressive liberals. I think they were rather proud of me. It gave them stature with their peers that I was gay. I never got into the dope scene. Somehow I feel I failed them there. My brother owns a plumbing business in Pasadena, belongs to the Better Business Bureau, the Rotary, Knights of Columbus, and I think he's a colonel in the Minute Men. I know he loved to shine the barrel of his rifle. How can I tell him he's still jerking off? He's on his fourth wife or maybe the fifth. I came by one Christmas to a party. He introduced me as 'My brother, the doctor. The only doctor, when you come to his office, you both drop your pants at the same time.'"

SIMON'S SOUL

The sponge stops for a moment to reabsorb the memory of that one. "I like working here. There's something very comforting in a prison. People have too many problems to worry about yours. Oh, some of the guards make dirty jokes about you, but it doesn't matter. A prison guard isn't the highest form of life. They're still evolving. The warden doesn't care who's screwing who, so long as he gets his cut of the action—you know, dope, women. Maybe you can't get out of here, Doctor, but it sure as hell is easy getting in. You want heroin, cocaine, acid—you want a blonde or a redhead, a white lady or a black fox—Christ, this place is busier than the L.A. airport. And the warden gets a cut of it. You told me about Heaven and Hell. I'm telling you you're in it right now. Only thing better about this one is no one judges you here."

He's serious now. This sponge is squeezing out a lifetime of fears, anxieties, frustrations. Like a deluge, thoughts tumble out, one onto the other. "I love God, Doctor, but I know He doesn't love me. God doesn't like fairies. I mean, I can hear Him say, 'I went to all that trouble to make men and women and you ignore them. Get out of my sight, you fruit.' I'm going to Hell, Doctor, and I'm afraid. I don't like pain. I believe every word you told me. Every damn word that damns me, and I'm afraid."

He believes me. And I believe him. He's right. It is better to be alive. Alive I can still make judgments. Dead I can only be judged. It comes upon me in hot, triumphant flashes, flooding me. My mind runneth over with the plan. A plan! Oh, what a glorious plan!

I will have to be careful, ever so careful, with Dr.

Stanley Shapiro

Roman. He is the key. I must make sure he will allow himself to be fitted into the lock and permit himself to be turned.

"It is true that you are going to Hell, Doctor." He stares at me, the sponge that absorbs again. "But I have a plan. If I should succeed, I may change your fate. If I succeed, you may be the first homosexual to enter Heaven."

It is wild, wild, an insane thought to mention to anyone, but heaven-shaking concepts were never meant for many ears. New worlds have always been discovered by the unloved, the unhappy, the unsure, the unrealized. Those with nothing to lose have never been afraid to risk what might be lost.

Dr. Roman, running his fingers over the Christ tattoo on his chest, sits, his two-legged body on the four-legged stool, and listens as I tell him my plan.

May 12 . . .

It is two weeks since I told him of my plan—two weeks since he gave me no answer. I had fantasized a simple yes and feared a simple no.

Twice daily he enters my room to tend to my physical injuries. I will not let him see the mental wounds his silence inflicts like so many mute daggers.

Two weeks I have suffered this reticent walrus, who takes temperature, pulse, and heartbeat from me and stores them in a corner closet of his mind, piled atop the tens of thousands of other temperatures, pulses, and heartbeats he has taken, hostages of his lifework.

He will sit there and study my face as though he

SIMON'S SOUL

expects my naked inner self to seep out through my pores for his physician's perusal. He will hold the knuckle of his forefinger between his teeth as he meditates. I want to scream out, "An answer! Yes or no!" But I must not press him as he sits in wrinkled thought. So long as he ponders, all is possible.

He has brought a chess set, and, wordlessly, we play. He is a superb chess master. My queens are so many fallen women to his bishops and his knights.

Does my lack of chessmanship hurry or hinder the verdict? Will he be loath to put his salvation into the hands of a man who cannot protect his king?

I will not beg the question, for begged questions usually bring forth poor answers. My time will come.

May 14 . . .

My time has come in the form of either a terrible humiliation he has suffered or some delectable sensuality he has reveled in. His blackened left eye is swollen shut, his cheekbone still puffed a purplish blue, the huge mustache bravely hiding a still-battered lip.

A balding balloon, he deflates onto the chair next to my bed. "You see, Doctor, a prison corridor is still safer than walking the streets."

He takes a yellow handkerchief from an inner pocket and touches his lip, leaving small red stains on the yellow background. Lips so tender his words rub raw across them.

"He was standing outside the hotel—and he smiled—and I followed him. It is not easy to walk away from beauty." His words are firm, demanding my attention, as he returns from the abyss of the night's shame to the morning's rage.

"I followed him to his room—and he opened his pants and allowed me to love him. And when he was done he pushed a badge into my face and yelled, 'Vice squad, you fucking fag,' and started to beat me up."

He pauses, the fury over the betrayal forming tears that rush down his cheeks and disappear into the thickets of his mustache. "He beat me until I was on the floor begging him not to hit me again. And he said, 'Lick my shoes, you stinking fairy.' And with my tongue still wet from his orgasm, I licked the leather of his shoes. . . . I hate them. I hate them all," he says bitterly, vindictively. Is he talking about vice officers, all officers, his brother, or the world's brothers in general?

"Hypocritical, deceitful, cruel bastards, all of them," he goes on to condemn them all. He pats his lips, coloring the handkerchief a deeper red. "None of them worth a shit, Doctor." And then, "I'm going to help you."

I say nothing. I'm afraid a word of mine might make him aware that I am one of the human race he hates.

"I'm going to help you escape, Doctor, and I hope you kill the whole fucking bunch of them."

He will help, not because he has faith in me but because he has no faith in them—in a world that has mocked him and driven him to a prison escape. I remain silent but silently bless the vice-squad officer who battered him.

May 17 . . .

SIMON'S SOUL

His medical reports have kept me in the hospital wing of the prison, but I am anything but a sick man. I am being fatted up, made ready. I will need my strength and my willpower, for this time there can be no backing down. I will have to stand firm in the face of pressures and horrors I cannot yet conceive.

He has handed me a key that will unlock the door to the room. I do not ask where he has gotten it from.

"Saturday night," he says softly as he puts the thermometer into my mouth. "When the women are brought in."

"The women?" I let the words slide down the thermometer to freedom.

"They bring them in on Saturday night," he answers in a reassuring whisper. "I told you, Doctor, you can buy anything here."

Prostitutes in prison. Are the pimps above the law, or are they the law? Is the vice squad the vice bringer?

"I've made the arrangements." His tones are hushed, but his temperament is turbulent. An emotional person by nature, he is becoming intoxicated by the passion of his revenge—the entrancement of giving the finger to the law that gave him the back of its hand.

"It cost three thousand dollars."

Money. I have thought of everything except what makes everything possible. Where do I get money? My funds are in my wife's keeping. I cannot wire for them. I cannot make a bank loan. I cannot go out and steal it. I am in despair. "I haven't got it."

"I didn't say it would cost three thousand dollars," he

corrects me, "I said it cost three thousand. It's been paid."

I have unquestioningly accepted the messiahship of his leading me out of this imprisoned land—but I can no longer control the urge to ask, "Why? Why are you doing all this?"

He removes his glasses and stares at me, and the two panda bears, no longer magnified, become two darting squirrels. "Because I believe in God, and it frightens me that he may exist."

NINETEEN

May 19 ...
It has cost three thousand dollars to arrange the escape. Money, money, God bless money. I once scorned it, but now I serve it. I have seen the Green Angel. I serve the Trinity—the dollar, the credit card, and the holy checkbook.

Oh, money, blessed money. Money gives, the lack of money taketh away. I pass out green pieces of printed paper and humanity grows food for me, feeds me, clothes me, services me, respects me, entertains me, protects me, loves me. Oh, money, you most sacred of earthly treasures, you most powerful of earthly weapons, you most godlike of earthly gods. You are there at the beginning and at the end. You are order. Your absence is chaos.

Three thousand dollars, like three thousand green knights, will bring down the prison walls.

11:30 P.M. ... The women were brought in. In what buildings, in what rooms they serviced the paying clientele, I am not sure—but at the half hour past the eleventh hour, the driver of the van who delivered them is feigning a heart attack. He is brought in on a stretcher to the room adjoining mine. The guards do not ask questions. All is done quietly, in haste. It would not do to have the news spread, for all are beneficiaries of these activites. Treat the sick man, then remove him as quickly as possible from the prison premises.

Dr. Roman, the only doctor on late-hour duty, applies mock resuscitation rites to the apparently stricken man. He tells the guard to secure additional medications. When the guard is gone, Dr. Roman knocks on the wall to my room. I remove the key that has been made to open the door that locks me in. I swiftly step out into the silent hall and relock the door to my room. Then a few steps to the adjoining room, where Dr. Roman and the stricken driver wait for me. I slide onto the gurney—not on it but right below it, where a small platform has been built about twelve inches in height. I slide in and the white sheet drops over the side, covering me. The guard returns with the medication, which Dr. Roman administers to the driver. Then, feeding him oxygen, they gently put him on top of the gurney. I lie on the panel directly under him, hidden from the guard's eye by the sheet. The guard then wheels the gurney down the corridors, past other guards, who open barred doors and look the other way. They have seen nothing. All the fringe benefits they derive from being guards depend on their seeing and hearing nothing. Just get the dying man out.

SIMON'S SOUL

Down a side elevator, to the van in which the ladies of the evening wait. One of the women will drive. The gurney, with the stricken man, is loaded into the van. Keep the gurney, just get rid of that heart attack—get off the prison grounds—it all never happened.

The wheels of the gurney fold under me as it is loaded into the van. I am cramped but comfortable between the folded wheels and the seemingly folded man.

The van starts to move. Seconds and yards pass beneath us. From slow movement, gears are shifted into higher speeds. Speed can only mean open road. I am free.

From what I can hear, most of the ladies are controlling near hysteria at being in a van with a dying man who breathes deeply of the oxygen cup on his face. A few of them utter banal consolations.

"You okay, Al?"

"Hang in there, baby."

"Keep breathing, honey."

"Gee, what a crappy thing to happen to a nice guy."

Some of the more realistic ones are concerned not for the man but for their money.

"Jeez, he was just about to come when this guard comes in and pulls him off. I think I ought to get paid anyway."

"That's right. We ain't been paid."

"Shit, couldn't he have waited a couple of more minutes before keelin' over?"

1:15 A.M. .... The van has stopped, and the grumbling, disillusioned ladies of a disastrous evening get out. To

Stanley Shapiro

what further delights of the night I do not know. The van starts up again, and I hear Al's voice. "Okay, fella, come on out." The white sheet is raised, and a hand helps me slide out of my cramped compartment.

Al is a rather thin, balding, innocuous man in his late forties, with bad body odor. He was born to be an accountant, spreading his mental sperm over big numbers, creating thousands of little numbers from them. What is he doing driving hookers into prisons? There's a story behind Al. I do not ask him for fear he will tell me.

"Where do you want to be dropped off, fella?"

"Dropped off?"

"Hey, the deal was to get you out of the slammer, then out of the van."

I do not panic. I have rehearsed the plan well. I know where I want to go. My house is in Brentwood.

2:05 A.M. . . . I am let off in the alley leading to the rear of my house, to Al's cryptic "Good luck, fella," but he offers no money to make that good luck come about. Born to be an accountant.

How very simple great escapes are. It's a good thing most criminals are more stupid than the police. It's what gets them caught. It's their mediocre minds, which plan improbable escapes, such as shooting their way out, that assure their staying in.

Oh, what a lovely escape. Hours from now the door to my prison-hospital room will be opened, and I will be gone, in an escape that will earn me a Houdini reputation. In the investigation that follows, no one will talk about a driver who delivered the Saturday-night pros-

SIMON'S SOUL

titutes and suffered a heart attack and was put into the room adjoining mine. And even if someone did privately discuss it, what would that have to do with my escape? Fear not, Dr. Roman, if it all works out, fairies may yet wear wings and play harps in Heaven as well as on earth.

In prison clothes I approach the rear of my house, the house that a thousand operations bought. Upstairs, the bedroom where my wife had brought me a thousand nights of pleasure. A good surgeon with a good wife. Why had I not been content with good? Why must a content man search for the reason behind contentment? Why must he try to dissect and analyze love and happiness? We don't break down the components of a good wine. We drink it and enjoy it. Why must we insist on knowing more than the moment needs?

No way anymore I can enter this house, go up to that bedroom, slide quietly into bed alongside my wife, and have her open her arms and legs to me. My lovely wife, my faithful wife, my good wife—there are duties in store for her other than wifely duties. She has not sought these other ways, but her very goodness has made her the most logical choice.

The spare house key is under the planter. It would not do for me to ring the doorbell. Even the best of wives may hesitate to open the door to a mass murderer who has just broken out of prison. Why confuse her? Why tear her between a wife's duties and a citizen's obligations?

The door opens to my known touch. Into the den. Why do they call it a den? Why this association with a pack of animals in jungle seclusion? My favorite brandy is still in the decanter. At least she hasn't destroyed it, smashing it in some fit of trying to forget the past—clearing the bar—opening her life to some man who favored other drinks. I pour the brandy into a glass and swallow. It enfolds me in a warm, soothing embrace. Oh, faithful liquid, you are good. That is enough. I do not want to take you apart—to the time you were a grape and some illiterate grower picked you and had you crushed beneath his feet. I do not want to think of you fermenting, of being bottled and shipped and sold. I do not want to think of what you will become, urine. You are good, and that is enough.

Across the living room. God, what it cost to put this room together. Why do we furnish living rooms and then sit in the den? Why do we buy thousand-dollar dresses and then wear blue jeans? Why do we buy huge insurance policies and then try to outlive them? Why do we purchase expensive burial crypts and then say the soul isn't in them?

Up the silent stairs to the second-floor landing. Why do we need second floors and second cars and second honeymoons and second chances? Is it because one lifetime makes us uneasy?

My son isn't at home. The absence of that wheezing snore signals the absence of that ingrate boor.

To the door of our bedroom. The tiny pale yellow night lamp is on. She sleeps on her side of the bed. It is difficult to break the habits of eighteen years.

What a lovely face. Good women sleep prettily. Breathing quietly, lips slightly parted, her golden hair sensuously covering part of her face, a few strands ever so

SIMON'S SOUL

gently wavering to her soft breaths. Her full breasts barely held in by the plunging lace nightgown. God forgive me for ever leaving her. God forgive me for coming back to her.

I mustn't wake her. Not tonight. On nights long past, I would stand by the bed and whisper to her, and the whisper would become a command far beyond her name itself. Her eyes and mouth would gently open in sleepy greeting to husband, lover, master.

"Ben, darling." Simple words but spoken in the intimacy of past intimacies. Oh, those glorious nights. She would raise herself to a sitting position and start to undo the belt of my trousers and draw the zipper down. Graceful, expert, loving fingers lowering my trousers and the shorts beneath them. Then testicles and penis were being held, stroked, fondled, and caressed. As she sat on the edge of the bed, her head would gracefully bend forward and her lips and tongue would draw me into her mouth. Then, as the hardness became rocklike and the head of my penis engorged and swollen, her hands would grab my buttocks and her head would wildly go back and forth, sucking the length of me, pulling back and taking me in again. Then the blind ecstasy of the orgasm.

And to the bathroom, where the hot shower was prepared, and as I stood beneath its warm, wet heat, she removed her nightgown and soaped, massaged, and washed me. And then, as though I were a Greek god, she reverently toweled me down. The stirrings within my loins as she lovingly dried my private parts and adoringly put lip kisses on them. And she was on her knees, then on

Stanley Shapiro

her back, her legs held high and wide, drawing me down to her, and I would enter to her cries of delight. Those lower lover's lips would part for my entrance and then come together to keep me from leaving, and each time I pulled out, drops of her wet excitement were on me. Faster and faster, her buttocks revolving in wild gyrations, her muscles drawing my penis in deeper and deeper, and then a taut stiffening and her screams as she came.

Oh, what nights. What a good wife. What a good way to spend the rest of my life, screwing you.

Quietly into the bathroom to the medicine chest. My things are still there. She has cast nothing out. Absolved from any physical or emotional commitment to me, released from any moral or spiritual obligation, she has kept my possessions, not to remind her of me but to remind her of her calling. She is a woman born to be kept by, and to keep, a man. Without a man to care for, she becomes a free-floating appendage, attached to nothing, useless. If she no longer belongs to a man, at least she can still belong to the man's possessions. There is identity in symbolism. It's why widows are still called Mrs. The day she meets the next man to serve, the moment her womanhood appendage attaches to his body and his protection, she would clean the house of my existence. Even the brandy bottle would not be spared. Her life would pour only from the new man's decanter.

2:25 A.M. ... I put on the rubber gloves, saturate the wad of cotton with chloroform, return to my sleeping wife's side, and hold the moistened fibers close to her face. The odorless fumes invade the unsuspecting body.

SIMON'S SOUL

Her heart beats, her lungs pump, her brain commanding them to beat and pump again. How vulnerable we are when we sleep, our very life depending on two small fleshly organs and the brain cells to direct them. Sleeping, we would not even be aware if heart and lungs failed. We simply wouldn't awaken, for the commanding brain would die if the commanded organs failed. What a sheer fishing line we haul our life's catch in on every morning.

2:27 A.M. . . . Her sleep is no longer natural. I lift the sheet from her and look. Whereas a body asleep can be sensual, a body unconscious is sterile. It is thought that gives credence to desire. A woman, taken to frenzied heights by her lover, if he should die—as he lay there naked—she might cry, hold his hand, kiss his cheek, but she would never grab his penis in her sorrow. Have you ever seen a man caress his dead wife's breasts or her vagina in his agony? Why is it obscene to fondle a dead sex organ but not a dead hand or dead lips? Because the fondled one is no longer aware of the gesture. Sex is not only in the eye of the beholder, it is in the mind of the beheld.

Her breasts, how helpless they stand, with no mind to tell them they are desirable. Her golden pubic hairs guard the entrance to a dead city, remaining at their posts, watching not over a raging fire but a forgotten flame.

2:32 A.M. . . . I have lifted her onto my shoulders and carried her down the stairs and out the kitchen door to the garage. As I open the rear door of the station wagon and, as delicately as I can, lay her down, a strange but not unknown excitement is building. The exhilaration one feels as he approaches a long-dreamed-of challenge. When

Stanley Shapiro

you are at the foot of Mt. Everest before the assault—when you step into the waters of the channel before you strike out for the other shore—when you sight the spoor of the giant tiger and know he is within gun range . . . Your head is flushed with the rushing of your blood, your muscles are taut in expectation, a current of energy propels you in dizzying momentum. I have felt it before, when we were about to kill Dr. Simon Warner and find his soul.

2:55 A.M. . . . I drive east through Beverly Hills. This city of banks and psychiatrists has become a wasteland of closed vaults and empty couches. Here and there a Rolls-Royce or Mercedes scurries through the deserted streets, the driver and the blonde at his side. Why are there always blondes in those large foreign cars, and why are the men always driving? Why aren't they at home doing what drivers and blondes are supposed to do?

What a desolate place it is at this dark hour. Not a shop, restaurant, building, or gas station open. This dream city wiped out by the reality of the hour. Beverly Hills, that beautiful balloon, blown up by the egos who enter it, deflating as they withdraw.

Up Coldwater Canyon, pitch-black, as the homeowners have turned off their lights and their hearts to the outside world. How can that many people sleep in that much darkness? Someone must be moving in those homes. Are they talking, quarreling, making love, going to the bathroom in the dark? Is it the chic thing to do, to turn off the lights? Is dark in and lights out?

Left on Mulholland Drive, where the absence of light is more than lonely, it is menacing. The headlights of the

SIMON'S SOUL

station wagon push long, white antennae ahead of us, like the white walking canes of the blind. They point the way and we go forward, without really seeing. The rearview mirror shows the blackness we just came through. The road is narrow, the wilderness ominous.

I am near it. I feel its melancholy presence. This ill-fated Spanish house that first felt the tortured steps of the recluse son and then the tortured soul of the recluse doctor. This millionaire's house, brought over piece by piece from Spain to house such pain. Its fate to shelter tears and terror, anxieties and abominations.

It stands black against the black sky, two unknowns blending into one sightlessness. The gate is held closed by a padlock and chain. With the doctor dead, with no relations, a will still being searched for, by the order of the probate court the house will stand untouched until the law decides how to divide the spoiled.

I smash at the fence with the station wagon's bumper and hood. The lock snaps. I drive across the gravel stones, mentally reliving the pain of their biting edges as on hands and knees I fled Hell's terror.

Out of the station wagon, around to a side window, and once again in Simon's house of horrors. I am sweating hotly in the chilled room. As I grope for the light switch I hear the floorboard creak behind me, hear the inhuman steps, and smell the rancid stench.

I am too terrified not to turn and face it. Terror multiplied can become blind heroism. I have seen it with soldiers; too frightened to become cowards, they become heroes.

I snap the switch, whirl, and face the coyote.

Stanley Shapiro

From recluse son to recluse doctor to recluse coyote. This house was not meant for good times. With the house abandoned these many months, an open door or window somewhere, the smell of man faded, the animal kingdom has come to reclaim its own.

It may be his land, but to me it is territorial imperative. I need it for immense deeds unknown to his simple needs. An inner instinct that has helped him survive centuries saves today for him. He turns and leaps out the window to the more friendly darkness.

The lights work. The first of many triumphs I will continue to need.

As much as I dislike most of our human race, it is strange how its total absence creates a sense of loss. Enter a home where someone sleeps and you still feel the warmth of banked fires. Enter a home where no one lives and you walk on cold ashes. How many unhappy couples have remained married rather than enter an empty house?

The door to the basement leads down to the surgery room. It is mad, this plan, but madness successful is genius. I cannot stop now. I have unlocked secrets so magnificent, so awesome, I have forfeited the right to say, "No more, no more."

I have seen too much to deny having seen. I have learned too much to deny knowing.

The surgery room is intact. The electronic machines, computers, instruments, monitoring devices, recorders, everything still there. By law nothing has been removed. One day it will all be sold, bloody item by bloody item, at

SIMON'S SOUL

some grisly auction attended by those purchasers of horror's mementos. Little after-dinner surprises. "Hey, folks, here's the ax the girl cut her folks up with."

"Gee, Lenny, you lucky stiff, where'd you get it?"

"Eighty-five bucks. See, there's still some dried blood on it."

"Jeez, I miss all the bargains."

"Honey, do you want some lemon chiffon pie?"

"Sure. Can I cut myself a piece with this ax?" (After-dinner laughter.)

3:55 A.M. ... I have carried my wife down into the surgery room, laid her on the table where Dr. Warner had been. I inject eight cc's of pentathol into a vein so she will remain unconscious while I prepare her.

# TWENTY

6:25 A.M. ... I have shaved her head.

Of all the punishments you can inflict on a woman, it is the grossest.

Her hair. Her blond, soft, sweet-smelling, living crown. The top point of the womanhood pyramid of hair, breasts, and vagina. The only woman part you could show. Breasts and vagina were for my eyes only, but her hair belonged to the world. Swept up, combed down, brushed out, it teased the world, reminding it of the other hidden golden garden of hair that it could never see.

Her head of hair, brushed one hundred times a night since she was five. The hair you grabbed in both fists as you drove deep into her. The hair that hung below her shoulders as, naked, she walked around the bedroom. Long blond hair and a well-shaped behind. Who could ask for anything more?

Her hair, which identified her as a woman long before pubic hairs grew or breasts developed. Her hair, the

SIMON'S SOUL

bedrock of her middle-class identity. Wash it, dry it, brush it, shape it, comb it. Lose your money, your friends, your health, your loved ones, but don't lose your hair.

It lay on the floor—thin golden umbilical cords that had attached the woman to her society. They lie in dead, drying heaps, no longer nourished by her body's juices. This lighthouse of her inner self, these arrogantly proud strands, suddenly no more than refuse to be swept up.

God forgive me, but it is the only way to reach You.

She lies there bald. She looks so helpless, so humiliated. It's shocking to see someone you love so thoroughly stripped of the dignity of their sex. I once had an English sheepdog and I wet him down with a hose, and suddenly he was no longer a full-haired, round-looking mini-bear but a thin, shivering, embarrassed mongrel. He stood there ashamed of his doghood. We are all so vulnerable, so easily stripped of the glowing outer shell that shelters the tiny force within it.

Was this naked-headed stranger the wife I had shared my life with for eighteen years? Does a head of hair a wife make? She has a truly well-shaped skull—but how can a man say to his wife, "Darling, you have a lovely skull"? On what grotesquely thin ground do we form lifelong relationships?

10:40 A.M. ... I have inserted the electrodes into the frontal and temporal lobes. I work as swiftly as experience and judgment will allow. All stereotaxic instruments, recorders, stimulators, and encephalograph monitors are functioning. The computer that houses the dictionary's words are now fed into her memory center.

Her thought center sends the words back in wave form. The waves are transferred from the electroencephalograph machine to the differential computer, which decodes the word from the wave.

I cannot bring you to conscious awareness just yet, dear wife. I am alone. There are so many machines to work. Conscious, even though strapped down, you might move, dislodging one of the delicate electrodes. I will explain after you are dead. I mustn't talk to you until it is too late for your talk to change my plan.

12:15 P.M. ... She is hooked onto the oxygen and blood machines. I shall turn them on. An irreversible process.

I wish it had been anyone but you, good wife, but your very goodness has made you the only possible choice. I am sure of you, not of a stranger.

You promised to love, honor, and cherish me. You cherished me well while things went well. You served me faithfully. Serve me this one last time. Belial's son is too wary to be caught again, but I can still catch Heaven's envoy.

I turn the machines on.

12:20 P.M. ... Her eyes move slightly. She is returning to consciousness. She will soon be aware. The needle finds her vein. I inject the twenty-five cc's of insulin.

One ... two ... three ... four ... five ... six ... seven ... eight ... nine ... ten. She is dead.

12:22 P.M. ... The computer sends her thoughts out.

"Where am I?"

"You're with me, darling."

SIMON'S SOUL

"Ben?" The computer cannot register emotion, just words.

"Yes, sweetheart, Ben."

"But you're in prison."

"I escaped."

"I can't see, Ben."

"Yes, I know."

"Or feel or hear or move."

"Don't be afraid, Catherine."

"Ben, what's happened to me? Where am I?"

"You're dead, Catherine."

There is no message for a moment, and then, "Oh, my God, I can't scream."

"Trust me, darling. There will be no pain."

"No! Please, God, no! I don't want to die.... Please, Ben, make me alive again."

"You're going to Heaven, Catherine."

"No, please, I want to go home.... Take me home, Ben, please." Then, in desperation, "I have a PTA meeting tomorrow."

A PTA meeting. I've done her a favor. "I can't bring you back, Catherine."

A pause, then, "I missed you, Ben. I never went out with another man, I swear it. I love you, Ben. You know I've always loved you. Bring me back, Ben, let me show you."

Oh, dear, good, faithful wife, even in death you wallow in middle-class values, in suburban rationale. You can't fuck your way back to life. You can't screw your way out of the grave. You are the victim and carrier of a social disease that places virginity above love, marriage above truth, family above fairness, promotion above philosophy, the corporation above compassion, a way of life above life itself.

Your hair is shorn, your lips are pale, your arms are stiff, your breasts are limp, your vagina cold. Hair, lips, arms, breasts, vagina—the very essence of you is gone. If you had lived on thought, emotion, philosophy, you could justify your return, but they who live by the body die with the body.

I still love you, dear wife. I wish you well. Heaven is worth dying for. Just serve God as faithfully as you served me. A Heaven full of good wives, Catherine. A Heaven full of PTA members, fine cooks, and careful drivers. Are their husbands in Hell? Is Heaven the final haven of widows?

12:29 P.M. . . . She has been dead for seven minutes but still will not accept it.

"I don't like being dead, Ben. It's dark and it's lonely."

"Be patient. Someone from Heaven will soon be coming for you."

"Ben, please, take me back. I'll do anything you tell me. Anything."

"I told you I can't. It's too late."

"I know. You're mad because I didn't write to you in prison. I was embarrassed, ashamed, confused. I thought you had killed all those people."

"I did, Catherine, the same as I killed you."

"Don't say I'm dead, Ben, please. Tell me I'm still alive.

SIMON'S SOUL

Tell me you'll help me. That's it. Ben, isn't it? You're angry with me and you're trying to scare me."

"Damn it, Catherine, you're dead. Do you want to come back to a rotting body? Your body is dead, all of it. It's beginning to decay, to stink."

Silence for a moment, then, "Does my body really smell, Ben?"

It is no time to soften the blow. "Yes, Catherine."

"Am I naked?"

"Yes, Catherine."

"Please cover my body, Ben."

I put a sheet over it. "It's covered."

"What do I look like dead, Ben? I mean, my face?"

"You're still beautiful."

"There's no blood or other things coming out of my mouth or nose, is there? Be honest."

"Nothing, nothing at all."

"Are my eyes open?"

"Yes."

"Are they still green?"

"Still green."

"Please close them, Ben."

I close them.

"Will you bury my body, Ben?"

"Later on."

"In a casket, like Ann Morrissey was buried in. You know, with the red velvet lining . . . Tell Reverend Foster I'd like the full choir . . . a lot of flowers, Ben. You know I love flowers. . . . Have Saks Fifth Avenue send someone out to dress me. I'd like a new dress, Ben. . . . And have

197

Charles make me up, but not to use a hair blower. It burns the hair and makes it brittle...."

Even in her death rites she has gotten caught up in her life rituals, her daily ministrations, missions, vanities, and vindictiveness. At this moment she is enjoying her death, her suffering. Death has become bearable as long as she is aware of it and treats it as she would a living misfortune.

"And, Ben, promise me you won't invite Ruth Henning to the funeral."

12:59 P.M. ... She has been dead for thirty-seven minutes. I have not told her I cut her hair off. To kill her is one thing. To be deliberately cruel is another. I have also not told her that I have drained the blood from her body. It would only make her extremely uncomfortable.

Having celebrated her wake long enough, she is again becoming panicked, and from chastened she becomes hateful.

"I don't want to be dead. I hate you, I hate you, I hate you."

"Do you feel anything, Catherine, like a curtain around you? Like someone or something beating on it?"

"I wouldn't tell you if I did. You had no right, no right to do this, Ben."

"Damn it, I'll cut off from you. I'll cut off and you'll have no one. You'll be alone."

The response is as I thought, fearful. "No, Ben, please don't leave me. I'll do whatever you tell me. I swear it. Don't leave me alone, Ben. I'm afraid."

"Do you feel anything around you?"

"Nothing. Just darkness."

SIMON'S SOUL

"A pulse beat, something?"

"Nothing."

It is too soon. I must not panic.

"What am I supposed to feel, Ben?"

"Be patient, Catherine."

"You said I was going to Heaven, Ben. You promised."

I am perspiring. I did indeed promise her Heaven. I want the darkness around her to dissolve into brilliant hues. I want the first beating against the curtain to be gentle and warm and loving. But what if I have misjudged her goodness? Outside of giving birth to our son, have there been any other dark deeds she has committed? While I was in surgery opening up a stranger, was she opening up to other strangers? While I saved, did she sin? I murdered her thinking her perfect. Am I responsible if she is less? Have I promised my wife Heaven and delivered her to Hell? It is done every day by husbands in other ways.

I pass from guilt to anger. This bitch, this full-hipped, soft-lipped bitch who led me down her sainthood path. I had banked everything on her goodness. Was my trust put into the wrong bank?

"Concentrate, Catherine. Pay attention. Do you feel anything? Anything?"

"I feel surrounded, Ben."

"Surrounded by what?"

"A curtain. A black curtain."

A black curtain. Simon's black curtain. Black. Hell's color.

"Catherine, I am going to be gone for a few minutes."

"No, don't leave me, I'm frightened."

"Just for a moment, dear. I'm very tired, very hungry, very thirsty. I need something to eat, to drink. I'll be right back. I promise."

Out the surgery room, down the long, narrow basement corridor, up the stairs into the empty room. It is empty of all furniture except for the telephone, which sits on the marble floor. I pick the receiver up and hear the buzz. It's still working. The phone, the electricity, the gas and water. I have known people who have had all four turned off when just a few weeks overdue with the payments. Here in a dead man's home they still service the unserviceable. Into how many dead addresses are they still sending living conveniences? I have got to sell my public utility stocks.

Into the Spanish den built for Spanish dons, now used by forest denizens. I snap the light on and hear the running steps of small creatures. The high overhead lamp cannot control the breadth of the full room. Light enough to see but still shadowed enough to make you look twice at what you see. In the best of times, uncomfortable—now, empty, dust-ridden, silent, it is forbidding.

The bourbon bottle sits on the bar top as I saw it the day of Dr. Warner's death. An army of police have been in this house, and it is as if no one has entered. A house where four incredible murders took place and the police have not left a trace of their presence. One poor Mexican doesn't pay a traffic ticket and they break in while he's in bed and shoot up the place. The law works in mysterious ways, but only if you're not white and not rich.

SIMON'S SOUL

I swallow two long gulps of bourbon. Damn, it's good. To hell with food and food for thought. To hell with man and man's best friend. There's still nothing that can solve your problem like a bottle of booze. Just relax, let it hit your gut and spread the good news.

As I raise the bottle to my lips I hear my dead wife calling to me from the basement. "Ben, where are you, Ben?"

TWENTY-ONE

I am frozen to the bottle I hold. I have seen the face of Hell, and it is not as terrifying as her voice coming from the surgery room below.

"I'll be right up, Ben. Don't go away."

Deep, dreadful chills shake my body. My clothes, wet from my perspiration, stick damply to my body. I can smell the sour sweat oozing out of my pores.

"Don't be afraid, Ben. There's just the two of us."

Through the shadows I can see the room beyond the den that leads to the basement door. I hear her coming up the staircase, one measured step at a time.

"I want to talk to you, Ben."

Her hand appears on the staircase handrail, then her shaved head. She hesitates, her face staring blindly at the ceiling, and calls, "Ben, where are you?"

Taking one careful, deliberate step at a time, she comes out of the basement, senses my direction, turns her body toward me. Her head lowers and her dead eyes fix on

SIMON'S SOUL

mine. Her mouth slowly forms a smile, an arm awkwardly lifts and points toward me. "There you are."

The bloodless hand pointing the way, the lifeless smile frozen in place, she methodically moves one leg at a time toward me. I cannot move to escape, whether in fear or fascination, in revulsion or stupefaction, I cannot say. I can flee from Hell's son, but I am paralyzed to flee from the mother of my son.

She is facing me. Tiny drops of blood mark where electrodes had been inserted into her skull. There is no reflection of myself in her pupils. Her eyes do not function, yet she sees.

"I am not angry with you, Ben."

Her fingers reach out and touch my cheek. I will retch or go mad. The voice comes from beyond the smile. "You were naughty, Ben, but I forgive you."

She puts her lips to my cheek and kisses me. My being will burst and I shall scream away my sanity. I bargained for God and Belial, for Heaven and Hell, but not for a dead wife's kiss. I survived the unthinkable demon—I would survive whatever Heaven could think to send, but . . .

Wait, wait, and wait again! I want to shout in jubilation, roar in exultation, leap to my deliverance.

Whatever Heaven could send!

Of course, of course, and of course again! That kiss. The touch of her flesh is warm—the breath she breathes is pure and sweet—the smell of her body is a thousand gentle fragrances—the voice as gentle and forgiving as a sleeping lamb.

"You are not my wife."

"No, Ben, I am not."

So blinded by the Hell forms, I did not recognize Heaven's fairness. I am delivered!

"My wife. Is Catherine in Heaven?"

"She is in Heaven."

Hosanna! Praise be! I have not killed my good wife in vain. Oh, Catherine, you were too steeped in everydayness, too filled with averageness, too committed to keeping things the way they were not to go to Heaven. You were incapable of thinking evil because you were wise enough to refuse to think.

"Her soul was due in Heaven, and you came to find out why it had not arrived," I say triumphantly.

"That is true."

"Now you are trapped in her remains."

"Yes, Ben, I am trapped."

Glory to God, I have caught God's glory! Not Belial's son, that raving, raging madness, but God's daughter, a loving, forgiving, peaceful serenity.

The room vibrates with her gentility. An unseen radiance erases the shadows, casting rainbow colors where only black and gray had reigned. From a distance there are the faint tones of musical notes, so wholesomely melodic I want to join in song and dance.

Gone is the den's tainted mustiness that held the house captive in its rank odor. A vinaigrette has been opened that fills the space with myrrh and attar, pomander and hyacinth.

As foul as is Hell's messenger, Heaven's envoy is as sweet.

SIMON'S SOUL

Dear wife, even after death your body continues to please me. It housed the earthly pleasures, and now it brings me Heaven's treasures.

"I must talk to you, Ben."

As she is learning to use the throat cords of my wife's voice, the sounds now float out silver-toned, each word a tuned note.

"You have created a problem, Ben."

Indeed I have, gentle lady.

"I cannot return to Heaven."

Oh, I feel so smug.

"If I do not return, it will upset the balance."

I cannot help it. She is so noble, so right, I do not want to mock her, but I must smile an arrogant, self-satisfied smile. "The balance?" I ask innocently.

There is concern in her voice, urgency. "If the balance is not kept, all will cease to exist, Ben."

Where have I heard that before? I step to the bar, find a dusted glass, wipe it clean with my fingers, and casually pour another drink. Urgency is Heaven and Hell's problem, not mine. I drink and swallow a pleased swallow. Oh, it feels so good, this game. I play my cards knowing each card is a trump. "And how do we correct this situation?"

"I must return, Ben."

"Can it be done?" Oh, such smug naïveté.

She has assumed control over my wife's body. Gracefully she walks toward a large leather chair. Catherine walked easily, but now her body steps with elegance. She seats herself in one fluid motion, her voice muted harp strings. "Yes, it can be done." She clasps her hands at the unpleasantness of the doing, but I will not let her off the hook I myself have dangled on for so long.

"How?" I demand the answer I already know.

"A soul was sent to Heaven—now one must be sent to—"

"To where?" Man commanding is man cruel.

Meekly she spins the word on a single silver thread. "Hell."

I pretend surprise and indignation. "You want me to send a soul to Hell?"

She does not look at me but merely nods her head.

"You want me to kill someone?"

She clenches her teeth, shivers, and nods her head again.

"Say it. You want me to kill someone."

"I can't."

I do not wish to hurt her but to hurt God, who has allowed Hell to be His equal. "Why should I commit a deed you find too repugnant to mention?" I pour another drink. "I want you to say to me, 'God wants you to kill.'"

She shakes her head.

"To kill is unforgivable, is it not?"

She nods.

"Yet God would let me kill to save Himself?"

She looks up at me. Her eyes are no longer dead eyes, nor Catherine's eyes. In her pupils are reflected images and colors I do not understand. There are moving figures and shades of ages too ancient to remember. "You do not understand, Ben," she says softly.

"How can I understand what I am not told? I only understand we are told not to fear death, and yet God

SIMON'S SOUL

cringes from it. We are told not to kill and yet God suggests it. I only understand I want a God who will honor His own Commandments." I then throw out the challenge. "I will not send another soul to Hell."

I see, for the first time, fear on her face. "But the balance."

"To heaven or to hell with the balance."

"There isn't much time, Ben."

I've heard that one before too. I use the bourbon's courage. "Time isn't my problem." I turn my back to her. "I'm going to Hell anyway. What do I lose if there is none to go to?" I throw out the bait with which I hope to catch Father Ryan's salvation. "If God wants me to save Him, there has to be a change in the agreement."

I am arguing with God's agent as one would with a salesman, with eternity no different than if a dishwasher were on the line.

Outside, a clap of thunder, and another. It is more than a dishwasher I am bargaining for.

She has risen and walked up behind me. Her words are feather soft but pressured. "It will all become nothing, Ben."

The rain coming down outside is coarse and polluted. Drops of stinking water smash against the windows, seeping in through the cracks. "Is that Heaven's rain or Hell's?"

"It is not Heaven's."

Belial is frightened too. He would devour me, rend me in a thousand ways, grind my bones to dust, and rebuild me into ten thousand monstrous forms, but my death would also be his. All he can do at the moment is throw

Stanley Shapiro

fear at me—but I have seen him and survived him. He will not defeat me now.

The thunder shakes the house; the torrent is bloodred. The wind circles with frenzied howls.

"Tell God to tell him to stop."

"He can't."

"What can He do?" I shout above the storm's savage roar. "I'll tell you what He has to do. I'll kill—I'll send a soul to Hell—but if I do, I demand an exchange—Father Ryan's soul to go to Heaven, one from Heaven to be sent to Hell."

"It can't be done, Ben." She doesn't raise her voice, but it rises above the outside madness. "There's never been an exchange."

She shall not be Isis revisited. "A soul exchange! Father Ryan's to go to Heaven!"

"It violates the agreement . . . the balance."

"A new agreement," I insist. "A new balance . . . A soul to Hell—Father Ryan to Heaven."

"If done, it might destroy everything."

"If not done, then everything is surely destroyed."

"It is dangerous."

"Why should the Hereafter be safer than today?"

"What soul, Ben? What soul already secure in Heaven should be sent to Hell?"

"Let God make that decision. A God should not be above making decisions."

"He promised them all eternal peace."

"Who will dare call Him liar?"

"It can't be done."

"Then His lack of will be done."

SIMON'S SOUL

"God mustn't die, Ben."

"I'm sorry, but my powers are limited."

A freezing, paralyzing wind—so cold the storm's putrescence is frozen solid. The walls are covered with a sooty frost. The molecules of air are iced and form ten thousand trillion frigid spheres. My flesh is a petrified sheet cracking into untold pieces. No breath to breathe, the air turned hard, frozen lungs are filled with a foul hail. A glaciated heart tries to pump congealed blood. And through the solid, frigid air comes the malevolent shriek, and the air parts like a frosted sea, and he is there, Belial's son.

The blood, covering head and body, a thick, stinking, iced mass—the pus from boils and sores pour slowly and fall like chunks of yellowish, decayed concrete. From open scars the gray smoke is a dense, poisoned cloud. Out of black holes where eyes and mouth should be, where once a red molten fire flowed, a cold, heavy sludge now seeps out. And from the arms, the frozen worms and maggots stick out of the holes like stone defilements—and the jagged claw a monstrous razor from which hang icicles of tainted blood.

It points its claw at me and howls its terrors, engulfing sanity in a thousand frozen maledictions. It swings the claw through rotted frost and roars an anger beyond abhorrence.

"Hurry, Ben, hurry." Her voice is immaculate amid the corruption.

I must not be beaten now. "A soul to be sent to Hell. Father Ryan's to go to Heaven."

It screeches its towering rage, and from its mouth pours

Stanley Shapiro

yellow urine and thick pieces of human excrement.

I will not be beaten now. "Father Ryan to go to Heaven, or Heaven and Hell to go to nothing."

Two terrifying claps of thunder and Belial's son and storm are gone. Two streaks of lightning, one silver-gold, the other an appalling reddish-black. They rush toward each other, wind around each other, but never touch. They back off and race toward each other again. They bend and circle, twist and turn, thrust and parry in ancient ritual. One final awesome thunder sound and lightning streaks are gone. I remain, shaking but standing.

In graceful cadence she speaks the glorious words. "It is agreed. An exchange of souls. One to be sent to Hell. Father Ryan's to be sent to Heaven."

Warm tears, human tears, earthly tears, stream from my eyes, some into my mouth and down my throat. How good happiness tastes. I have beaten Heaven and Hell. I have faced up to God and Belial and faced them down. Superior to the greatest of creatures in how they live, but equal only to the lowliest in that they want to live.

Bear your suffering but a moment more, Father Ryan. Soon you will be in Heaven. All it takes is one more murder. Soon you will bend your loyal Irish knee to your God, and He will say, "Aye, and it was worth changing the rules to have you with us, Father."

"It must be done now, Ben, now." For the first time her crystal voice shows slight cracks of anxiety.

I turn to her, having come too far to fail, having been too tested to trust. "How do I know they will keep their word?"

SIMON'S SOUL

"God never lies, Ben."

"But what of Hell? It is conceived of lies."

"It will honor its promise."

"I have only Heaven's word for it. What about Hell's?"

I see him sitting in the corner, almost lost in the dark green wingback chair—the little black boy, whom I last saw as thirteen pieces of burning flesh. His hands rest on his knees, palms upward. One palm the purest gold, the other, ten thousand jagged, twisting, stinking crevices. The symbol of the balance. When the balance changes, will he change too? Will he become a white, freckle-faced, blue-eyed lad?

He will point out the soul to go to Hell.

TWENTY-TWO

2:15 P.M. . . .
I have taken a gray worsted suit from Dr. Warner's closet for myself and a beige trench coat to cover my wife's body. The boy will remain in basic black.

Simon's car is still in the garage, the keys above the visor. I am in the driver's seat, my wife's body next to me, and the boy sits by the window. The battery, which has uncomplainingly sat out the months on its metal island, turns the engine over at first asking. Is it a Die-Hard battery serving another trio of diehards?

We drive down the snakelike canyon, east on fabled Sunset Boulevard, and onto the faded Sunset strip. Yesterday's glamour, today's gonorrhea. Fire-trap bars hustled by naked waitresses, food parlors that reach culinary peaks if they turn out a grilled hamburger, record shops and variety shops, cleaning stores and unclean stores, shaded gas stations and shady motels. The sidewalks hold a human stew—runaways, aging hippies, hookers and

SIMON'S SOUL

those they hook, the zonked in and the spaced out, the Levied straights and the leathered gays. Big dreams and small deals.

The walking debris do not even stare at us. An escaped murderer sitting in a car with his dead bald-headed wife and a black boy who is part Heaven, part Hell. We are not an unusual threesome in this area.

Left into the hills again. Not Beverly Hills but the cheaper hills.

One more isolated, single death. That soul to be the key that I will insert into Hell's lock to force open its gates. Father Ryan will step out, his faith in God made purer still by the ghastly fires. When he emerges, will other souls race out to freedom like shorn, singed lambs from the slaughter? Dr. Carlson, Dr. Blakely, Dr. Mannis, Dr. Warner. Is Dr. Mannis' Jewishness a plus or a minus there? Is Dr. Blakely's madness a curse or a blessing there? Is Dr. Warner's white Anglo-Saxon courage appreciated or tested?

2:40 P.M. . . . The hillside homes are modest in price and architecture. Boxes that will stand—set into the unresistant but resilient earth. It can bide its time until these little boxes collapse from earthquake, fire, flood, or their poor design.

I glance at my wife's body but feel no revulsion, no guilt. The Catherine I knew is in Heaven. Does her soul feel a sense of loss for this body she tended and cared for over those forty-two years? Like a naked turtle, she has been taken from her shell and delivered to her God. If I had seen the real Catherine, the naked Catherine, without her shell, would I have married her? Do we purchase the design of the car or the engine that drives it? And this engine that is now driving my wife's body, this force within her fleshworks, was it once human too—is it divine energy, a heavenly spirit, a fragment of the Godhead? If I were to stop the car and embrace my wife's body, would this force feel my hands on my wife's skin? Would it feel desire, or is there nothing to desire in Heaven?

I am heading in the direction I feel the boy would like me to go. I have traveled death's road with him before. I know it is forward of me, but having stood up to Heaven and Hell, surely I can stand up to their double agent.

"What is your name, boy?"

No answer. I know black people don't like to be called boy. I try again. "What is your name, sir?"

"He cannot speak," she says.

"Has he a name?"

"Yes, but it cannot be mentioned."

"Do you know it?"

"Yes, but it was never told to me."

"How can you know what wasn't told you?"

"There is no need to be told what is known."

I start to argue but hold back. It is true. No one ever tells us how to breathe or laugh or cry or drink or chew food. We just know.

"Can he hear or feel?"

"Neither. Nor can he see or think."

I object. "But he has pointed out people for me to kill."

"He never saw them."

SIMON'S SOUL

It is true, all true. We go through life without our senses. People cry out in loneliness, we do not hear them. They suffer, we do not feel for them. They despair in front of us, we do not see them. They need us, we do not think of them.

Like an immense jigsaw puzzle, little disturbing pieces keep falling into place.

3:00 P.M. ... The black boy's sightless eye sees the gray brick house just off the bend of the road. He nods his head.

I pull to a stop behind the green Thunderbird. The boy points to the car. Whoever has the pink slip to that car has but moments to live.

The Thunderbird! That noisy bird with the gold-plated hubcaps, silver-chromed mufflers, and a license plate that reads BIGGIE. It is my son's car!

TWENTY-THREE

My son to be my final victim! My wife and now my son. Is this black boy choosing or being told to choose? Is he Machiavellian in his muteness, or is he merely a lifeless puppet moved by some distant ironic hand?

The irony is mine. My pulse races to keep abreast of the laughter rolling out of me. My son! That offensive, insensitive, ungrateful beast. That rapacious, self-indulgent, big-cocked brute. That hulk without a mind. That penis without a conscience.

How often, when I have seen him sulking at the dinner table, shoveling inflated cuts of my money's meat into his thankless stomach—how often as he sat there consuming our budget, without throwing us a scrap of a word, a crumb of a glance—how often as I heard his larded body stumbling around his bedroom, emitting gigantic farts into newly washed sheets, pissing loudly into the open-doored john with an arrogance that perceived it to be holy water—how often when he tossed lipstick-stained shorts

SIMON'S SOUL

onto my laundry bill, when my light bulbs lit the way for his insolent eyes, when my furnace heated his callous body, my rugs stained by his plodding boots—how often have I yearned to lock my surgeon's fingers around his gross neck and press until his offensive breath no longer polluted home or planet.

In through an open kitchen window, onto the sink and then to the floor. I hear a woman moaning from a nearby bathroom. It is not the moan of normal pain but of pleasant pain.

Into the small, cluttered living room, its decor empty beer cans, a shirt, bra, pants, and underpants. The woman's voice is louder, her moans becoming deep, incoherent groans.

The walls are covered with unframed photos of scuba divers, power boats, and lonely reefs. The underwater spear gun hangs in a place of prominence. I take it down, set the steel shaft in place.

The woman is on her knees in her bed, her rear thrust high into the air. He stands behind her, driving his enormous tool into her. With each thrust she now screams, "Oh, God, oh, God." He is indeed her god. She is indeed in his heaven. Long, incoherent sobs, and she is crying out, "I love you, I love you," into unhearing, uncaring ears and heart. He stands, emotionless, behind her, curiously watching her heated frenzy.

Do I hate him because he is a shit or because he is a shit with a huge cock? Would he be less reprehensible if he were less endowed? Am I merely jealous or merely judging?

"Oh, Jesus," she screams, and her body jerks in the orgasm. Impaled on his mighty sword, she thrashes about helplessly, breaks down, and cries as the second wave of pleasure inundates her.

My son-of-a-bitch son, the insensitive tyrant, yawns.

I raise the spear gun. "Tommy, you bastard!"

The woman, riding the crest of her passion, does not hear me but continues to cry and moan and scream, twisting her sweated bottom.

My son turns his piggish eyes to me, then steps back a long step, to enable himself to pull free his Goliath.

Lost in the intensity of her orgasms, the woman continues to pump her buttocks, unaware that the flesh that drove her there is no longer guiding her.

He stands in dumbness, oxlike behind his erection. With a penis over a foot in length, six inches in circumference, my son is a bedroom knight you do not joust with. He will win your fair lady by either your default or her deceit. Little matter to her that behind the suit of armor a dwarf exists. She will pierce her honor on his lance. Given enough years to live, he will spread great joy and greater sorrow. A lucrative short-term investment, a long-range bankruptcy.

"I killed your mother."

"How'd you get out of jail?"

His mother's death has dropped short of his loyalty like a spent arrow. His only concern is how my presence affects him.

"Ingrate! Slob!" I yell. "I just told you I killed your mother. Cry for her memory. Pray for her soul. Make believe you care."

SIMON'S SOUL

The woman in bed is staring at me stupidly. It is not her fault. It's hard to look intelligent when you are on your knees with your ass sticking up in the air.

No tears roll from my son's eyes. No facial sign of remorse or loss. His mother's death is a message, not a blow. I am the Dr. Frankenstein who conceived this monster. I put a rotted seed into my good wife, and her belly distended with the weight of his unworthiness. He came into the world sucking its air, and he has taken ever since.

"I'm sending you to Hell, you cold motherfucker," I shout. "Hell is cuntless, you miserable shit. Your cock will be cut off slice by stinking slice."

His lips part and his broad teeth show in unbrushed sarcasm. "You've done enough killing, fella," he says as he takes a step toward me, his hand and his penis preceding him. "Let's have that spear now, huh?"

My God, this idiot has reached deep into the memory banks of a mind that was weaned on television. He's pulling a John Wayne or a Clint Eastwood on me. It doesn't matter which—that sort of arrogance spans all generations.

The steel shaft pierces his body. The woman in bed screams. The animal grunts—looks at the metal to which cling pieces of his heart—stares at me with a newfound respect. His penis slowly starts to lower. His life flag is coming down.

He dies standing up.

As he falls to the floor, the woman screams again and again.

It is balanced. God and Belial will live.

Stanley Shapiro

I run out of the house to the car as the woman's screams bring others out of other houses. Into the car and we are gone.

At sixty miles an hour down the hill toward the city where three like us can get lost. My wife is in Heaven, my son is in Hell, just Father Ryan and all will be well.

As I harshly twist the steering wheel from left to right and left again, the screeching tires are all I have to tell me if I am still on the road. My wife's body falls forward and bounces from side to side. A dreadful stench comes from her. I understand. What was in her body is now back in Heaven. But why is the black boy sitting so composed while my wife decomposes? Why hasn't he broken into burning pieces? Why is he still with me? He pointed out my son, his job is done. Or is it? Has it to do with Father Ryan? Are they trying to back down? "The exchange," I yell as I jerk the steering wheel that jerks four tons of steel. "They promised."

The boy nods.

"A soul to go to Hell. Father Ryan's to go to Heaven"

The boy nods again.

"Has it been done?"

He shakes his head no.

"Will it be done?"

He nods.

"When?" I am shouting. "I must know when."

He answers with a black hand that points. I steer madly toward the pointed way.

TWENTY-FOUR

We have driven into the cemetery off Melrose Boulevard. It is empty except for the silent stones that mark the noisy past. Where are today's mourners of yesterday? We sing the songs of yesterday, tell its jokes, buy its possessions—why don't we honor those who made it all possible?

The boy gets out of the car. I follow. We walk past six new dug holes, not yet filled by the coming coffins. Six of them. A plane crash? A gang war? A polygamist who had a family argument?

He stops by two gravestones. He holds his pure palm up for me to see and points to one of the gravestones. I understand. "That one went to Heaven."

He holds up his corrupted hand and points to the other stone. I respond, "And that one went to Hell."

He then closes his Hell palm, opens it, and I see Father Ryan's living face in it. Father Ryan in Hell.

He then closes his Heaven palm, opens it, and I see Catherine's face. My wife in Heaven.

He then closes his Hell fist and puts it into Heaven, then closes his Heaven fist and puts it into Hell.

"No," I cry out, trembling, "it's not fair, not fair."

Oh, you all-knowing gods, how humanly cunning you are. Oh, immortal gods, how true to life are your ways. Oh, high-and-mighty gods, what lowly choices you offer man.

I am in turmoil. "They will make the exchange. Father Ryan's soul to go to Heaven, my wife's soul to go to Hell."

The boy nods.

"Not fair," I say again in my anguish. "Not the two I love. Another choice. Give me another choice. All I ask is fairness."

The messenger of the gods stands silent. He sees no fairness, speaks no fairness, hears no fairness.

They will break the promise by breaking my heart. They will back down by having me back out. "It is unfair, unfair," I shout to the empty heavens. "You are making me choose the impossible choice."

The boy holds both hands high in the air. Between the Hell palm and the Heaven palm float the faces of Father Ryan and my wife. I must choose or forfeit.

"I choose," I yell. "I choose . . . I choose . . ." I am torn by unbreakable loyalties to both. "I choose to speak to them first. A word with them and then my decision," I demand. "I have earned the right. I ask for one moment of eternity's time. A word with them and then my decision."

SIMON'S SOUL

I am driven to my knees by a crushing silence. It obliterates the sound of the rustle of a tree leaf, the shifting of a grain of sand, the breath of an insect. A silence so intense I hold my ears to keep them from bursting outward into the vacuum of this dreadful aphonia.

My wife's face, floating between the boy's palms, begins to glow in beauteous coruscation. Her golden hair shimmers in dazzling effulgence. Her smile is eye-blindingly resplendent. The voice that comes from her throat is honey flowing from a silver sea.

"Thank you, Ben. Thank you for delivering me."

"I'm sorry I had to kill you, Catherine."

"You didn't kill me, Ben. You opened the door to my God."

"Are you content, Catherine?"

"I have seen Him, Ben. I am with Him. It is beyond happiness, beyond love, it is glory forever."

"And if I had the power to take you from there?"

"No, Ben, please. It would be a damnation I could never survive. Let me be, Ben. I am so happy ... so happy ... so happy."

Her face becomes shadows hovering between the boy's hands—and Father Ryan's face is framed in hueless shades, obscured, tenebrous tones of harsh, lurid tints. His face is swollen, distorted, ravaged by an unbearable, intolerable suffering. Repellent sores and gashes all but blot out the features that gave his face familiarity. He howls and wails in horrendous, convulsive pain.

"Forgive me. Forgive me, Father Ryan." Hot tears of

anguish roll down my cheeks. "It is I who sent you to Hell."

"It is my doing," he shrieks through the excruciation. "I offended the God I love."

"What was your sin?"

"I don't know . . . I don't know . . . But I have sinned."

In Hell, not aware of why, he loves the God who sent him there. "I can get you to Heaven, Father, but a soul would have to be sent from there to Hell in exchange."

"No," comes back the valiant reply. "Send no one here. It is unendurable. Oh, my God, how I suffer."

"I cannot leave you there forever."

"Yes, if forever is my God's will."

His face recedes to hanging in the balance between the boy's hands.

"I choose," I cry out in anger, despair, frustration, rage, "I choose Father Ryan . . . to remain in Hell."

You are too noble a soul, Father Ryan. Heaven cannot hold your love. Heaven is for the good, not the gifted. Heaven is for the ordinary, not the outstanding. For you God was a cause, for Catherine a duty. For you, to serve Him was an obsession, for her an obligation. While you yearned for God, she earned God.

Father Ryan's face is pulled into the Hell palm, my wife into Heaven's. The black boy splits up the middle, the halves held together by brilliant bolts of crackling energy, and then each half is sucked into a different gravestone.

I race through the cemetery, not sure of where to stop and face Him—the spot of confrontation always just a bit

SIMON'S SOUL

farther on—and the earth round, we come back to the beginning and run on—circling all our lives, searching for the God ground.

I stumble and fall to the earth in exhaustion, my face in the burial dirt. I thirsted for answers and I have ended up drinking the damp earth.

"Oh, God," I sob in my agony, "I am sorry I ever searched for Simon's soul and found it. Sorry, sorry, sorry. It is better to believe in an uncertainty, with hope for the future, than in a certainty with no hope at all. What have I gained by finding a God who will say no to me?"

"Oh, God, I am so confused. Why couldn't you have been as magnificent as our beliefs? Why have you made it so difficult?"

Inaudibly at first—a faint pealing at the start—it grows into a wondrous roar that stuns and makes servile. Face in the ground, I grovel, laughing and crying. My tears wet the earth. It is God! It is God come to explain. And I hear God's voice say, "Don't move, Dr. Reynolds, or I'll shoot."

I lift my tear-stained, dirt-smeared face and look up to the police helicopter.

TWENTY-FIVE

June 12 . . .

I am in a cell with bars beyond bars, guards beyond guards. I told them how I escaped, how I killed my wife to trap God's messenger, how I made the deal to keep Heaven and Hell from vanishing if Father Ryan were sent to Heaven, how I killed my son to maintain the balance, how God and Belial tricked me, how I decided to keep my wife in Heaven and leave Father Ryan in Hell . . . I told them everything. No one believes me. I send letters asking when I will be paroled. No one answers. I send letters to civil-rights lawyers; they come back unopened.

I am no longer concerned with the soul and the Hereafter—only possessed to understand the earthly atoms that compose us. How to disassemble and reassemble them again. I have progressed to a point where, last night, I was able to put my arm through the cell walls up to my elbow.

SIMON'S SOUL

In the event that I ever decide to escape again—since Hell is my destiny and I have nothing to lose—I have made a list of all those I feel should be sent there as soon as possible.

It is an intriguing idea.